THE MERGING

LAS VEGAS PARANORMAL POLICE DEPARTMENT
BOOK ONE

JOHN P. LOGSDON

CHRISTOPHER P. YOUNG

CRIMSON MYTH
PRESS

Published by: Crimson Myth Press (www.CrimsonMyth.com)

Cover art: Audrey Logsdon (www.AudreyLogsdon.com)

Thanks to *The Merging* Reader Team!
(listed in alphabetical order by first name)

Aaron Paden, Adam Goldstein, Adam Saunders-Pederick, Allen Stark, Amy Robertson, Andrew Greeson, Antoinette Hilton, Beth Marsch, Bonnie Dale Keck, Brandy Dalton, Caroline Watson, Carolyn Fielding, Carolyn Jean Evans, Cassandra Hall, Charlotte Johnston, Dan Sippel, Davina Noble, Debbie Tily, Del Mitchell, Denise King, Diann Pustay, Hal Bass, Helen Day, Ian Nick Tarry, Jacky Oxley, Jamie Gray, Jan Gray, Jef Ball, Jennifer Reinhardt, Jess Thorson, Jessica A. Lopez, Jodie Stackowiak, Joe Simon, John Debnam, Kate Smith, Kathryne Nield, Katya Gordon, Kevin Frost, Laura Thomas-port, Louise Thompson, Lynette Wood, Lynne DeBoer Moody, Marie Boucher, Marie McCraney, Mark Beech, Mark Brown, Martha Hayes, MaryAnn Sims, Megan McBrien, Mike Helas, Natalie Fallon, Noah Sturdevant, Noel Hera, Pam Elmes, Patricia Wellfare, Paula Pruitt Jackson, Paulette Kilgore, Penny Campbell-Myhill, Ruth Nield, Sandee Lloyd, Sara Pateman, Sarah Newton, Scott Ackermann, Scott Reid, Sian Johnson, Soobee Dewson, Stacey Mann, Stephanie Claypoole, Stephen Bagwell, Tara Parry, Teresa Cattrall Ferguson, Wendy Schindler.

CHAPTER 1

There are plenty of things to do in Las Vegas on any given night, but chasing a rogue vampire through town doesn't show up on any of the pamphlets. At least none that I've seen.

"Ian," said Rachel Cress, my partner since joining the Las Vegas Paranormal Police Department, better known as the Las Vegas PPD, "tell me he's at least done something truly nefarious."

Her sapphire eyes glistened against her pale skin. Today's hairstyle was blond with braids here and there. The look was perfect on the backdrop of her brown leather outfit. When she got her hands glowing with magical energy, it was all I could do to keep my libido in check. But I had to control myself. There was a time where Rachel and I were peers in the force. We were allowed to play with each other back then. Well, technically we weren't, but we did anyway. Actually, pretty much everyone on the squad did because we were the only ones who truly understood what it was like being in the PPD. Five years ago, though, I was promoted to chief. When that happened, I swore off having relations with anyone on my crew because, well, it just wouldn't be right. I still said inappropriate things... a lot, but everyone understood that was due to my genetic make up and so they let it slide. I was a horndog, plain and simple. Of course, so was everyone in the PPD. It was a side-effect of our genetic engineering.

"He bit a normal," I replied while taking a turn toward the Bellagio.

"Any other normals witness it?"

"Nothing reported," I answered.

"So he'll get a couple years at the most," Rachel said with a grunt.

"Plus rehab."

I pulled over to the side of the road and took a look around.

There were plenty of normals walking about, laughing and generally having a good time. We lived among them, worked among them, and even vacationed among them. But whenever one of our kind flipped into full vampire or werewolf mode, the normals filtered it out. That filter was easily demolished by magical battles or a direct attack, much like the one done by the vampire we were hunting, but most of the time normals were oblivious.

Fortunately, we had a public relations firm built specifically to handle situations where supernaturals intruded. They were called The Spin, and their job was to make normals believe that these mystical situations were all part of the Vegas experience. Unfortunately, the regional owner of The Spin was one Paula Rose, an ex-girlfriend. What can I say? I have a thing for normals. Not that I don't have a thing for supernaturals, but there's something about normals that really got my engines revving. Rachel suggested it had something to do with their being less of a challenge. I found quite the opposite to be true.

I spotted Mr. Vampire seated on the ledge by the water feature, looking sated. Guilty, but satisfied.

"*Cleared to move, Lydia?*" I asked through the connector, a device all PPD officers had implanted to allow communication between home base and other officers.

"*All set, baby,*" she replied in her sweet, ultra-perfect voice.

"*Thank you, love,*" I replied, giving a wink to Rachel at the same time.

"You're sick, you know that?"

I loved pressing Rachel's buttons. "What?"

"What?" she mocked while strapping a knife to the outside of her boot. Rachel was the only mage I knew who resorted to weaponry if the magic failed. It made complete sense to me to have a backup, but most mages are a bit snobbish about things like that. "The rest of us get the pedantic drone of Lydia's artificial intelligence. You get a phone-sex operator."

I shook my head and snapped up a fresh magazine for my gun, making sure the contents were infused with wood fragments.

Some myths *were* true, after all.

Wood for the vampires and silver for the werewolves.

The bullets I had were called breakers. They'd been developed specifically for use by members of the PPD.

Dastardly things, too. They exploded on impact, driving shards of your favorite monster-killing materials throughout your target in the process.

"Jealous much?" I said before opening the door.

She scoffed and rolled her eyes. "Yes, I'm jealous of a computer. When was the last time you got laid by something non-mechanical?"

"Ouch."

"Is that what you said during it?" Then she pulled the handle and exited the car. I laughed and batted my eyelashes at her. "What's the plan?"

I'm sure we both hoped the perpetrator would decide to fight. It'd been a while since we'd seen any real action.

It all depended on the kind of drunk we were dealing with. When a vampire breaks down and bites into a normal, they either get power-mad or they get laid back. It was a dice roll to know which one you'd get. Being that we were in Vegas, dice rolls were apropos.

"I'll take left," I said, jogging to the other side of the street so that Rachel and I could flank him.

The light was waning but I could see in near blackness. It was one of the many traits of an amalgamite.

Our vampire was seated in the little alcove near the center of the Bellagio's water feature.

When vampires drank blood, it was like they'd downed quite a few shots of whiskey. They got plastered, and that meant they were either lovey, sulky, or power-hungry and violent. From the looks of our perp, I would have guessed he was a calm drunk. Or at least not a violent one. A single kill was rare for those seeking a power rush, after all. This guy appeared to be sulking.

"*I'm clear,*" I said through the connector, crossing the street a ways down and then cutting back, keeping my gun out but tucked by my side.

"*Moving in,*" Rachel replied through the connector.

The way she moved reminded me of a lioness. Lithe, smooth, and deadly.

Her hands glowed, signaling she was prepping for a light show.

Between her magic and my bullets, this poor vampire was a goner, assuming he didn't surrender.

He only had two exits: bolt straight ahead or cut through the fountains.

Whatever his move, we'd catch him eventually.

We always did.

There was a time early on when the job had been a challenge, but Rachel and I had gotten so good that taking down your standard vampire or werewolf was almost mundane. A gang of them could be fun, but singles were just too damn easy.

"*Don't blow up everything,*" I warned Rachel as I thought about how The Spin was already going to have to explain how this vampire sank his teeth into a normal. "*The last thing I need is Paula on my ass about having to handle public relations on account of a magical battle outside of the Bellagio.*"

"*Says the guy who wants to start using a fifty-caliber Desert Eagle,*" Rachel replied.

I grinned at the thought. "*But I'm not using one, am I?*"

"*You will.*"

Our vampire pal had clearly taken notice of us. He stood and began fidgeting.

"Get your hands up," I called out before he made any

decisions. He paused, giving me the opportunity to try the moderately-nice-cop routine. "Look, pal," I said gently, "I don't want to have to shoot you, but I will. And if I miss, that mage over there will wreak all sorts of havoc on your flesh in order to give me time to try again."

He looked at Rachel, whose hands were bouncing little bolts of lightning back and forth between them. Then he turned back at me.

"Doesn't have to go bad, buddy," I said, keeping the gun pointed at his chest while continuing to close in. "You're already in a world of hurt. Don't bring any more normals into this and you'll be out in no time." I motioned with the gun. "Just put your hands up and I won't unleash a bath of wood fragments throughout your body."

His hands slowly went up as he gulped.

"I didn't mean to do it," he said desperately. "I just..."

"I'm sure you didn't," I replied, having heard the excuse a hundred times. "Chomping into a normal's neck just happens sometimes. We've all been there."

"You've done it, too?" he said, looking downright pathetic.

"Well, no," I replied, relaxing slightly. "I'm not a vampire. I just meant that we've all screwed up at some point."

"Idiot," Rachel said.

I shot her a look, frowned, and said, "Get down on your knees."

"Excuse me?" she replied, her head tilting my way.

"No, I meant for *him* to..." I coughed and then repeated my command directly at Mr. Vampire.

He slowly lowered himself down.

"Dammit," Rachel hissed, clearly displeased over the fact that there'd be no firefight.

We were within a few feet of him when we noticed a look of instant terror on his face.

His eyes opened wide milliseconds before I heard a growl and felt a blow crush against my right shoulder.

The pain ripped through my body as I landed a good ten feet away.

My head buzzed and my vision was blurred. Whatever the hell just clobbered me had some major power.

Screams and growls filled the area as my mental cobwebs began to clear.

I pushed myself up, shaking my head while reaching out to grab my gun.

When I looked over, I saw a werewolf tearing our vampire pal to bits. It wasn't your standard werewolf either. This one was easily a full head taller than any naughty doggie I'd seen before, and it was much thicker. Besides, he was ripping through a vampire like it was nothing. That's not an easy thing to do.

My brain was having difficulty processing the entire scene.

It just made no sense.

The power of the werewolf was incredible, as was its ferocity.

I'd been on the force for seven years and I thought I'd seen everything.

This was something new.

It solidified my desire to pick up that Desert Eagle the next time I was selecting weaponry.

That's when I realized that Rachel had gone quiet.

I scanned the area.

She was lying limp on the ground off to the beast's right.

"Rachel," I called out, taking a wobbly step toward her.

The werewolf spun and looked at me like a jackal does a fallen antelope. His red eyes glowed as blood dripped from his teeth and claws. A rumbling growl radiated from him, signaling he had no desire to be friends.

"Not good," I said, pulling up my gun and firing it repeatedly.

Wood-imbued breakers wouldn't do much to kill the damned thing, but I had no time to load silvers. I just hoped they'd hurt enough to make him run.

It worked.

He ran like hell.

Unfortunately, he was running directly at me.

CHAPTER 2

I went to dive out of the way, but I was still a bit wobbly and so only managed to fall over.

This worked to my advantage since Fido, Rex, Spot, or whatever the hell his name was, had obviously expected me to side-step. He jumped where I was planning to dive and flew right past me.

"Dammit," he growled as I fumbled for a mag of silver breakers.

There was no way I was going to get them snapped in place before he reached me, but he didn't know that. I smacked the bottom of the gun and leveled it at him. The chamber was completely empty, so it was going to take a bit of acting to convince this guy.

He paused and squinted at me.

"Come on, big boy," I said in as menacing a voice as possible. "I'm sure that silvers will cause you a bit more discomfort than woods."

"You have no idea what you're up against," he said, glaring.

"Then why are you hesitating?"

That's when a flash of light flew past me and smacked Fido on the side.

Rachel was back up and she was pissed. Fireballs were flying from her hands like it was her last hurrah.

Paula from The Spin was going to have a field day trying to explain this one to the masses.

The wolf howled as he bolted at me. I pulled the trigger multiple times before remembering there were no actual bullets in the chamber.

"Shit," was all I could say before he knocked me on my ass, bringing with him a mass of flaming fur.

I was expecting the worst, but I looked up to see nothing but sky.

Rachel was screaming and firing at our new buddy as he dived into the water. The flames on his fur were quenched immediately as Rachel ran toward the ledge.

"Rachel," I called out before she could leap in after him, "you're not going to catch him that way."

She stopped pre-dive and let out a frustrated cry as she fired off more magic than I'd ever seen. It was to the point where she looked like a glowing orb of pain and death.

I knew she was running on pure adrenaline at this point because there's no way she could have released that much magic without it dropping her. She was genetically enhanced to be able to unleash more power before tiring than your average mage; it was all part of the gig at becoming an officer in the PPD, but there was only so much in the tank. I'm sure she had another fifteen minutes in her if she'd been running at a normal clip, but there was too much flowing from her fingers.

"Rachel!" I yelled a few times before she finally realized what she was doing.

She stopped, panting.

"Sorry," she said finally. "Lost my head."

I helped her off the ledge as we watched Fido continue along his merry way.

"That's the fastest damn doggy-paddle I've ever seen," I said as I watched him go. "That dog could be in the Olympics."

"We have to get to the other side before he gets away," she replied, staggering slightly.

"You've overdone it already, Rachel. I'm sure you've got more energy, but he clobbered you pretty good."

"I'll be fine."

She took a step toward the car and nearly fell over.

"Yeah," I said, catching her and dragging her to the rest of the way, "you look great. Just get in and rest. I'll call for backup."

Rachel was out the moment she hit the seat.

I knew she'd be pissed that she wasn't part of the kill on this guy, but there was no point in her being on the scene in this condition. She'd just be a liability.

"*Lydia,*" I called through the connector, "*we've got a big bad wolf at the Bellagio. He just shredded a vampire, knocked me and Rachel around like we were nothing, and then he took off across the water.*"

"*Oh my,*" she replied. "*Are you okay, sweetie?*"

"*A little cut up, but you know I heal quickly.*"

"*Good. I don't know what I'd do without you, lover.*"

Okay, so maybe it *was* a little weird for the PPD's AI to consider me her lover.

I glanced down at my partner. *"Rachel's wiped out, but she'll be okay."*

"That's nice," said Lydia with an edge. *"I'm assuming you need backup?"*

"Fast."

I cracked the windows and chirped the security system on the car before running around the far edge of the building.

My wounds were already healing and my head was almost fully cleared. One of the many nice things about being an amalgamite was having fast recovery. There was also the incredibly dense bone structure, base magical powers, supernatural strength, lightning-fast reflexes, the ability to lower my heart rate so I could keep my weapon leveled and steady, and countless other things. I wasn't a vampire or a werewolf or a mage or any of the other multitudes of monsters that lived among the populace of the world. I was a combination of them all. It wasn't like I was the top-of-the-line model of each, though. I had to use all my skills together to be effective. There were a few special abilities I possessed that I was aware of and, based upon the fact that I'd mostly stumbled upon those, I assumed I'd discover more.

Also, I was the only amalgamite in existence. Or, if there were more, nobody seemed to know about them.

Essentially, I was born defective... in a good way.

"Should have brought the car," I said as I rounded the final corner and spotted the massive werewolf licking its wounds.

It looked up at the clacking of my shoes against the concrete. I really needed to start wearing sneakers or at least rubberize the bottom of my fancy footwear.

"Hands up, Fido," I called out, raising my gun before remembering that I'd still not inserted the mag.

"Fido?" he said with a wince. "That's insulting."

I furrowed my brow, glancing past the sights of the gun.

That's when I realized what I'd said aloud. Thinking such a thing was bad enough, but it was even worse to actually say it.

"You're right," I said apologetically while slowly moving forward. "Sorry about that. Just the heat of the moment and all, you know?"

"Whatever you say, Fang," he shot back.

I stood up straight at that verbal slap.

"I'm not a vampire. Why does everyone think I'm a vampire?"

He sniffed the air. "What the hell are you, then?"

"An amalgamite."

"Wait," he said, blinking. "Are you telling me that I'm facing Ian Dex? *The* Ian Dex?"

I couldn't help but feel a little pride at hearing my name spoken with such wonderment. I'd heard "Ian, Ian" many times over my years, and more than once I'd even been called "God," but that was in an entirely different context.

"In the flesh," I replied proudly.

His teeth showed and he began laughing. It was just a slow rumble at first, but then it turned into a full belly-laugh that was somewhat unnerving. Pretty soon he had his hands on his knees while his cackling continued.

"What?" I said, feeling suddenly confused.

It took him a few moments to gather himself, but then he looked around and tilted his head like a dog who had just heard a funny noise.

"Where's your mage?" he asked while wiping his eyes.

"She wore herself out casting spells at you," I answered without thinking, "so I put her in the car and… shit!"

His eyes locked in on my car and he jumped back in the water and began his speed-paddle back toward Rachel.

"You've got to be fucking kidding me," I yelled as I spun on my heel and took off again, this time making sure I had a silver chambered.

CHAPTER 3

*B*y the time I got to the other side of the building, the sound of a car alarm filled the area. I picked up my pace, but I knew there was no way I was going to catch up to him in time.

Sure enough, Fido had smashed the window, hot-wired my Aston Martin, and sped off with Rachel.

"Son of a bitch," I yelled. *"Lydia, where the hell is my backup?"*

"They should be there any second, puddin'. Everything okay?"

"No, everything is not okay," I said as a blue '68 Camaro SS pulled up.

"Climb in the back, Chief," said Jasmine Katrell, another mage on the force.

When it came to appearance, she was the antithesis of Rachel. She was still gorgeous, but instead of the blond-haired, blue-eyed look, she had the black-hair, emerald-eyes thing going. She *did* wear the standard mage leathers though. Sitting next to her, in the driver's seat, was Felicia Logan, a dark-skinned beauty with deep brown eyes who also happened to be a werewolf.

PPD officers were set into pairs with one being a mage and one being some other supernatural. It was more about practicality than diversity. Sticking two mages together *could* work, but there were only so many solid mages in the world who found police work interesting, which meant we had to place them carefully.

And, yes, *I* was the chief of the Las Vegas PPD, which would undoubtedly make you think that I'd know better than to divulge to a crazed werewolf that my partner was exhausted and sitting alone in my car. In my defense, he'd caught me off guard by mentioning my name and then laughing at me.

Felicia was spinning out her tires before I could even get situated. This made for a fun game of me bouncing around in the back seat.

"Lydia's got your car tracking," Jasmine said over her shoulder.

"We'll be on them in a sec," Felicia said, cutting a corner so tight that my head slammed against the window.

"Ow," I said.

"Please don't break my glass, Chief," Felicia said. "It's getting harder and harder to find replacement parts these days."

I moved behind her and braced myself for the next turn, gripping the sides of her chair in the process.

Up ahead was my red Aston Martin. Fido had the windows down with one arm out as he zipped along,

almost teasing me with the fact that he'd swiped my car…
and my partner.

From what I could see, Rachel was still out. That was
good, at least.

"Get me close so I can stick a silver in his head," I said,
using a growl that even Fido would be proud of.

"While he's driving, Chief?" Felicia asked in such a way
that I had to check myself.

"Well, no," I replied, "but at the next stoplight or
something."

Jasmine looked back with a face that noted the
stupidity of my statement.

"You think he'll stop?"

I groaned and checked my gun. "Just catch the guy,
will ya?"

Felicia's Camaro was closing in as Fido took another
turn that put him on East Flamingo. He was trying to get
back to Las Vegas Boulevard.

"Can't this thing go any faster?" I asked as calmly as
possible.

"Hold on," Felicia said and then gunned it.

There was something to be said about the roaring of
an engine in a muscle car. It was power personified. The
rush of caveman grunts that filled the base of my brain
was on overload as the engine rumbled furiously.

We pulled up to the right of my car as I rolled down
the window and got my gun at the ready. I couldn't shoot
him, as the ladies had pointed out, but maybe the threat of
me firing would be enough to make him second guess his
next move.

"Pull over, asshole," I called out, pointing the gun at his face.

He did something we didn't expect.

He slammed on the brakes.

CHAPTER 4

*T*he Camaro SS squealed like an angry pig as Felicia locked up the tires, sliding us halfway across Las Vegas Boulevard in the process.

Fortunately for us, it had been a green light.

I spun around and spotted Fido doing a three-point turn.

Without thinking, I reached out the window and pulled the handle on the door, pushing Jasmine's seat forward and climbing out of the car.

"A little notice would be nice next time, Chief," Jasmine said as the seat slammed back into position.

"Oh, sorry," I replied before I started running toward Fido.

He was backing up to complete his turn when I shot out both tires on the driver's side. He clearly knew that he wouldn't get anywhere fast with that because he abandoned the car with an enraged howl, leaving Rachel safely behind.

"Felicia, check Rachel," I commanded through the

connector as I chased Fido down the access road between Bally's and the corner Starbucks. *"Jasmine, get to the other side of the access road to Bally's. We've got to corner this guy."*

"Ian, sweetie," Lydia broke in, *"there's another disturbance down on the old strip."*

I was barely able to keep my voice steady. Amalgamite or not, chasing down an uber werewolf was damn tough. My eyes were jumping all over the place to make sure that he wasn't about to jump out at me from some dark corner. Fortunately, I caught sight of him padding down toward the other exit.

"Can't be as bad as this one," I said through panting breaths.

"Chuck says it's a vampire unlike any he's ever seen, puddin'," she replied.

"Patch him in," I stated as Fido slowed up, clearly spotting Jasmine as she walked into the opening of the access street with hands glowing.

"Hey, Chief," Chuck said, *"we got a vampire here who is pretty badass."*

"How badass?" I asked, hoping it wasn't anything like Fido.

Seven years of relative ease being completely interrupted in a single night sounded like a Pandora's Box waiting to be opened.

"Never seen the like," he answered. *"He's been throwing stuff around a lot. I unloaded a set of wood breakers into him."*

"Did it have any effect?"

"Yeah, he threw a Mercedes at my head."

That wasn't good. *"Oh."*

"Griff has been doing everything he can just to stop the guy

from destroying the Nugget," Chuck continued. *"He's only got so much magic in the tank, though."*

"*Swell,*" I said. *"Try to get the guy underground and away from the normals. We'll be there as soon as we can."*

I shut down the connection to Chuck and refocused on my current prey.

Fido was obviously seeking an escape route, but I wasn't about to let him get away again. Diplomacy worked some of the time, sure, but other times you had to take more drastic action.

So I cracked off a round, striking his thigh and eliciting a scream of pain in the process.

He spun at me with rage in his eyes.

I fired again, planting a silver through the shin of his other leg. He fell forward as Jasmine hit him with a bolt of energy, throwing him flat on his face.

It looked painful enough, but something told me he was playing at a ruse because this had gotten too easy. If what Chuck said was true about the vampire being equivalent to our friendly little werewolf here, my silvers were probably not doing nearly as much as he let on. Still, I don't care how powerful someone is, holes in the leg make walking difficult.

I re-aimed at his forehead and closed the distance, realizing that there was no way this guy was going to let us take him in.

"What the hell are you?" I asked as I got closer.

"Your worst nightmare," he replied.

"Oh, come on," said Jasmine as she cautiously edged around the beast. "That's just dumb. 'Your worst nightmare?' Really?"

Fido looked up and grimaced. "What's wrong with that? I thought it sounded rather tough."

"Sure, if you're in the fifth grade," Jasmine mocked. "It's too cliche. You need something that's yours, you know?"

He pushed up to his elbows. "Like what?"

"I don't know," she replied. "How about something like, 'I'm the beast who will rip your soul from your flesh' or something."

"That's not bad," Fido stated, looking impressed. "Mind if I use it?"

"Be my guest," Jasmine said with a shrug. "Might want to hurry up, though. I don't think things are going well for you at the moment."

The beast laughed heartily at that.

He was moving slowly toward Jasmine with each laugh. I caught it before he could get any closer.

"Oh no you don't," I said, pulling Jasmine back while keeping my gun trained on our werewolf pal. "He's playing you, Jasmine. He did it to me once already."

Fido glared at me moments before he slammed his hands into the ground and pushed himself to full height.

The bullet wounds on his legs were still visible, but they were almost fully healed.

I fired off a round into his chest, which staggered him for a moment but only seemed to anger him more.

Amalgamite or not, I didn't think I could handle a full-on assault from Fido, so I unloaded the rest of the bullets into his head as Jasmine peppered him with ice shards.

He fell backward with a sickening thud.

While Fido may have somehow been immune to silver,

his brain wasn't immune to being separated from his skull.

We waited as the werewolf effect wore off, revealing the body of the actual person who had taken this form. He wore a black suit and white shirt that marked him as one of the executives on the strip. His head was mostly gone, but his wallet was still intact.

I cracked it open.

"Richard Brenkin," I said.

"Fitting name," Jasmine chimed in.

"Huh?"

"Richard," she said with a shrug. "Think about it."

I groaned at her.

"*Lydia,*" I said, calling back to base, "*can you pull up a file on a Richard Brenkin?*"

"*Richard Brenkin is an executive in the finance department at the Bellagio hotel. He has no family on record.*"

"*Okay,*" I said while flapping his ID against the palm of my hand. "*Please notify the supers at the Bellagio that one of their own went rogue and had to be taken down.*"

"*You got it, sugar.*"

A van pulled into the access road on one side as Felicia's blue Camaro closed in on the other.

The neon letters painted on the van read, "The Spin."

Paula Rose stepped out wearing her standard business attire. She had that librarian thing going on. It gave me the shivers, but now wasn't the time for pleasantries.

"What the hell's going on, Ian?" she stormed. "I've got people posting videos on the net of a werewolf ripping apart a vampire, running across the Bellagio pool, and then coming back."

"He was dog paddling, actually," I started.

She just stared at me with her arms crossed. "How the hell am I supposed to spin this?"

"The dog paddle? I don't know. I guess I'd say that..."

"I'm talking about the entire scene, you hunk of coal."

"Your job, not mine," I replied with a frown. I then jumped into the back of Felicia's car. "I've got enough trouble to deal with. This guy was the toughest werewolf I've ever seen and apparently he's got a vampire buddy on the old strip who is being just as difficult."

"Another one?" she yelled out as the Camaro pulled away.

CHAPTER 5

*R*achel was coming back to consciousness as Felicia gunned the accelerator toward the old strip.

"What happened?" she said and then looked around, touching the leather seat in front of her. "And why are we in Felicia's car?"

"Long story," I said, trying to deflect.

Rachel was one of those people who managed to forget the fifty times you saved her ass due to the one time you did something stupid, like getting her kidnapped by a werewolf, for example. But as long as we kept our heads in the game, there was a solid chance it would all blow over and she'd possibly even forget about it.

"The chief chased after the werewolf, missed, and the werewolf came back and kidnapped you," Jasmine called back from the front.

"Thanks, Jasmine," I said with a grimace, feeling a sudden sense of dread.

Rachel slowly tilted her head my way. "You what?"

"It turned out fine," I said, waving my hand as I did my best not to look her in the eyes. "Uh… he's dead. You're not. All good."

Rachel stared at me with her mouth agape.

Finally, she said, "Unbelievable."

The ride to the old strip was somewhat quiet aside from the incessant growl of the Camaro's engine and the silent berating that I knew Rachel was giving me via the confines of her thoughts. I couldn't read her thoughts, no, but I could feel the irritation from the other side of the back seat.

It was so thick that I scooted as far from her as possible.

I tried to take my mind off of things by loading up a fresh set of wood breakers. Supposedly we'd be facing a vampire that was similar to the werewolf we'd just left, so having a new mag loaded was a good idea.

Rachel had moved from her silent thoughts to mumbling to herself while shaking her head a lot. If I didn't take care of this soon, those grumbles would get louder and louder.

"It's not like I did it on purpose," I whispered, trying to keep the conversation between us. "I thought you'd be safe in the car as I went around to take care of Fido."

"Fido?" she said, hanging on to something else that pointed out she disapproved of my actions. "That's just wrong."

"If you had seen him laugh at me after learning who I was, you'd feel different."

"You told him who you were?" she asked, not bothering to keep her voice low. "When did this happen?"

"When I caught up to him around the back of the Bellagio."

"Was this before or after he kidnapped me?"

"Before," I admitted. "He asked where you were and I explained that you were back in the car, too exhausted to…"

I stopped and gulped, realizing that I just admitted to every stupid thing I managed to do during my interaction with Fido.

"Unbelievable," she repeated, looking very disappointed indeed.

But this wasn't fair. Yes, I screwed up. Big time. But it wasn't like she was some perfect princess who did everything right.

"Now, don't you go getting all high and mighty on me," I said in my defense. "Lest you forget that time there was a gang of mages causing all sorts of mayhem near Harrah's, and when I thought you had my back I found that you were busily making out with an old flame who happened to be a part of the gang."

She shifted uncomfortably as both Jasmine and Felicia glanced back with their jaws hanging in disbelief.

"Yeah, that's right," I said, nodding my head defiantly. "Don't let her little innocent act fool you. She's quite naughty when she wants to be. Just like that night we were stuck on surveillance and she…"

I stopped again.

If looks could kill, Rachel's glare would have had me

six feet under already. Tack on to that how Jasmine's disbelieving stare bore into my soul while Felicia's glare via the rearview mirror threatened to char my flesh, and I knew that I was in a world of trouble.

"You slept with her, too?" asked Jasmine coolly.

"Wait," Felicia said moments later. "You slept with both of them *and* me?"

"Not all at once, obviously," I replied, finding a way to make matters worse. And then, just to really drive home my idiocy, I added, "That sounds pretty awesome, though."

Their glares were even worse now.

Rachel tilted her head at me even farther. "Have you slept with everyone at the PPD?"

"*He hasn't been with me,*" said Lydia, her voice sharing that same tone of irritation.

"Well, Ian," Rachel pressed, "have you?"

"Not *everyone*," I answered, sensing it was safer to own up than to clam up. "I'm not into dudes."

They all face-palmed.

"You're warped," Jasmine said.

"Very disappointing," agreed Felicia.

Rachel shook her head. "Seriously."

The air in the car was like iron.

Was it my fault that all of them were incredibly hot? No.

Was it my fault that they all came on to me at one point? No.

Was it my fault that I took advantage of the fact that they'd come on to me at one point? Well, yeah, but... again, they were all hot!

Finally, the voice of Lydia broke through the connector.

"*I forgive you, sweetie.*"

"You would," said Rachel.

"Okay, okay," I said, hoping to put a stop to this. "It takes two to tango, remember? It's not like I did this by myself. You were all involved. Individually, I mean." They didn't reply. "Besides, that was five years ago! I haven't been with anyone on the force since becoming chief and you know it. And are you all honestly telling me that you've not slept with anyone but me on the force?"

Jasmine and Rachel glanced at each other and then quickly looked away.

"Oh, no way," I said with a laugh. "You two hooked up?"

They said nothing, but Felicia's head snapped toward Jasmine. "You didn't."

"It was a stakeout," Jasmine admitted. "You and Chuck had gone out for coffee and one thing led to another."

"*Excuse me,*" said Chuck through the connector, indicating that they were on full broadcast mode, "*but while you guys are all talking about your sex lives, Griff and I have our hands full with a vampire who is doing his best to destroy the Golden Nugget.*"

"*We're almost there,*" replied Felicia as we turned onto Freemont.

I saw this as an opportunity to divert the conversation. "*Are you underground yet, Chuck?*"

"*Sorry, Chief,*" Chuck answered. "*He wouldn't go, but we did get him on top of the building. Sort of.*"

"*Sort of?*"

"He climbed up there on his own."

"Why?"

"You gotta see it to believe it, Chief."

CHAPTER 6

*A*s the Camaro turned on South Casino Boulevard, I stuck my head out the window and glanced at the top of the Golden Nugget. I didn't see any action, so I was hopeful that Griff was keeping his spells to a minimum. If he was unleashing hell, we'd have seen the glows against the night sky.

Felicia pulled into the hotel entrance and we all jumped out.

One of the security staff was at the main door waiting for us. I flipped open my badge and she stepped aside while putting a call in through her walkie-talkie. They'd obviously been expecting us.

Only those with proper training would see us in our supernatural form, which none of us were currently sporting anyway.

Technically, I didn't have a particular look beyond my standard one, and the mages didn't change either, unless you counted glowing hands and eyes, of course. The werewolves, vampires, fae, pixies, and so on were a different story completely.

The one thing that all hotel staff were taught to recognize, though, were the PPD badges. Some knew what we represented, most didn't. Regardless, they all cooperated with us when we came through. If they didn't they'd be looking for new employment. This had to do with the layout of the big cities and how the supernaturals interacted with the normals. The majority of executives throughout the world were supernaturals. You could tell who was and who wasn't most of the time. If the CEO of a corporation was a complete asshole, you could rest assured they were a normal. The execs were the ones who ultimately funded the Paranormal Police Department, and The Spin. It was good business to keep the normals in the dark as much as possible.

Another guard ushered us through a set of doors that led to a special elevator. He stuck in a key and pressed a button that was hidden behind a small door that had popped open.

My knees nearly buckled at the speed the lift shot up.

When it slowed and the doors began to part, I put a hand on the guard's shoulder and told him to stay back.

"We're on the roof," I said through the connector.

"It's about time," replied Chuck. *"We're on the East Bridger side,"* he said, indicating the road that ran alongside the Nugget.

We padded across the building and jumped onto the connected roof, fanning out as we cleared the choke point.

Across the way I spotted Chuck in his black overcoat

with the matching brimmed hat. Griff was kneeling on the opposite side, keeping the glow of his hands low while giving off enough light to reveal that he was wearing leathers.

Mages, I thought derisively with a shake of my head.

The vampire was facing away from us all, standing on the edge of the roof with his arms pushed out dramatically.

"Come to me, minions of the night," he was yelling. "Join the truth, the edge, the life!"

"What the shit is he talking about?" I asked to nobody in particular, now understanding why Chuck said I had to see it to believe it.

There stood an overlarge vampire, hands up in the air, calling down to the old strip that he was seeking followers. For what, I didn't have any clue, but I couldn't imagine he was seeking friends to join him in starting up a pottery club.

"No idea, Chief," Chuck answered. "He's been doing this since we followed him up here."

The vampire was easily as large as Fido had been.

Where they'd come from, or whatever spell they were under, or whatever infected them... it was obviously having an impact. I could only hope there weren't many more of them roaming the streets because we didn't have the bandwidth to handle this sort of mayhem.

"What's he done so far?" I asked. "Aside from this 'calling to his minions' thing, I mean."

In response, Chuck pointed down at the top of the Nugget's parking lot. There were cars flipped upside down, a few hanging precariously near the edge, and one sticking out of the side of the building.

"*He* did that?" I asked with an incredulous look while pointing at the vampire on the ledge.

"Yep."

"Swell."

I unholstered my gun and checked the magazine again, just in case. I usually wasn't this OCD about things, but Fido and Captain Vampire were throwing me a bit off my game. It didn't help that the ladies on the force were all holding grudges against me at the moment either.

But I wasn't worried about them.

I paused.

Okay, maybe I *was* worried about them. Fortunately, they were professionals who would do their jobs *before* making my life miserable.

"*Get ready, everyone,*" I commanded through the connector. "*I have a feeling this isn't going to be fun.*"

CHAPTER 7

*O*nce I was sure everyone was in place, I took a deep breath and approached the humongous vampire.

"Excuse me," I said, keeping a few steps back. He glanced over his shoulder. "Sorry to interrupt your minion-calling, but I was hoping you might come with us down to the station and step inside one of our fine cells?"

He turned back away and began laughing. It was a genuine laugh. Much like the one Fido had used behind the Bellagio.

"You must be Ian Dex," he said in his deep, booming voice.

"That's right," I said, feeling somewhat confused at how he knew that. "And you are?"

"Your master, should you choose to follow me," he replied. "I shall take any vampire who wishes to join me."

"I'm not a vampire," I said. Then I looked at my crew. "Seriously, why does everyone think I'm a vampire?"

The big vampire spun around and studied me from

head to toe. "You don't give off a werewolf vibe," he said and then pointed at Felicia, "like that one does."

I shook my head. "I'm not a werewolf either."

"Well, mages don't typically carry guns," he stated with a nod at my firearm.

"I'm an amalgamite."

He squinted. "Sorry?"

"Wait a second," I said, choosing not to answer directly. "You know my name is Ian Dex, but you don't know that I'm an amalgamite? Are they only providing basic information in the bad-guys pamphlets these days or something?"

"It's rather elementary, my dear Mr. Dex," he said with a voice so calm and condescending that it made me feel like a schoolchild who was about to be taught a lesson. "You are from the PPD, yes?"

I squared my shoulders. "Obviously."

"And you are the *head* of the PPD, true?"

"Well, yeah."

"And how many times in the last seven years have you been on *SN-50 News* to talk about supernatural crimes against normals?"

"Oh," I said, feeling somewhat sheepish. How was I supposed to know this guy watched the news? "Well, okay then."

"Feeling better now?" he said with a dull look.

I shifted but kept my gun low.

If this didn't need to turn into a firefight, all the better. My gut told me there wasn't much chance of this going easy, but at least it was obvious that this vampire hadn't had any blood recently. He was too clear-headed.

"Much. Thanks."

"No problem."

"Anyway, pal," I said while trying to act like I was just doing my job, "you made a bit of a mess here and we're going to have to run you in."

He nodded slowly as he scanned each member of the squad. They all had their weapons drawn or their hands glowing, except for me. I was trying to be the voice of reason.

"I think not," he said finally before turning back to summon more of his flock.

I could only hope that none of his followers, assuming he had any, were actually heading this way.

Just in case, I glanced over the side of the building and saw nothing but a few onlookers who were pointing and laughing. They likely assumed it was just another silly performance being attempted in the middle of the night. With the number of times The Spin used that particular explanation, it was a wonder anyone would think supernaturals existed at all in the heart of Las Vegas.

"All right, buddy," I said in a commanding voice, "I really don't want to have to resort to violence, so if you wouldn't mind…"

He turned around again and took two giant steps toward me until we were standing face to face.

More accurately, we were face to chest. My face, his chest.

Like I said, he was a big dude.

"I will give you one chance to leave here, Mr. Dex," he whispered in a voice laced with menace. "If you choose to bother me again, we will learn what it takes to kill an amalgamite. Are we clear?"

I slowly raised my eyes up until they met his. It wasn't easy acting tough in situations like this, but part of my genetic make-up apparently had an issue with being bullied. I just didn't like it.

"Oh, we're clear," I said as I emptied my gun into his groin.

CHAPTER 8

*T*he look on his face was priceless as he dropped to the ground, clutching the spot his manhood used to call home.

I jumped back as a scream of pain bellowed from deep within his soul.

His visage was a mix of rage, hate, fear, and murder. It reminded me a bit of the look Paula Rose had on the night I broke up with her a few years back, with the difference being that she was clutching my manhood and I was the one screaming in pain.

"Damn, Chief," said Chuck with wide eyes as I continued backing away, "you just shot the dude in the cock."

"That was rather unpleasant to watch," pointed out Griff.

"You haven't gone one-on-one with one of these things yet," I shot back in my defense. "You've been hanging back. Trust me, blowing his dick off was a smart move."

"That sounded wrong," noted Jasmine.

"If what you say is true, hotshot," Rachel chimed in, "why does he look even bigger than before?"

She was right.

It was like the opposite of the Samson story. Where Samson lost his power after getting his hair chopped off, this guy looked to be gaining power at getting his pecker blistered with wood breakers (which seemed rather fitting).

"Damn," I said as I struggled to reload my gun.

With a ferocious yell, the vampire launched through the air at me, swinging a menacing fist at my head in the process.

Magic knocked him away before he could rock my world.

Again, the ladies on my team may have been holding an underlying grudge against me that it'd take weeks to live down, but they were good cops.

The vampire's hand snaked out and caught hold of my ankle, ripping me off my feet. I landed with a thud as he began dragging me to the edge of the building. I could survive a lot of things, but I wasn't immortal. A fall from this high up would make for one of those naps I didn't wake up from.

It was Griff's turn to join the fun. He unleashed a shock spell that shook the vampire and me to the core.

The vampire let go of my leg before reaching the edge of the building, but the pain that convulsed through my bones made me wish he'd been able to drop me. It hurt so damn bad that I couldn't even groan. Imagine having a tooth pulled by a proctologist, using the standard entry path proctologists were known for, and you'll get the general idea of the kind of pain I'm talking about here.

Shots were firing and magic balls of light were crushing the vampire as I lay there in anguish, waiting for the contractions to stop.

As soon as things died down, Griff came back to me and cast a small incantation that stopped the shock spell. Then he leaned down and looked me over.

The tiredness on his face indicated how much effort he'd expelled in saving my life.

"Thanks," I said as another wave of pain raced through my body, "I think."

He obviously noticed my discomfort. "It'll pass in a few minutes. I apologize, but there was no other way."

"Is he…" I groaned as my back spasmed. "Is he dead?"

"Quite," Griff answered.

My breathing was gradually returning to normal. I pushed myself up on one elbow.

The vampire was a mess. He was riddled with enough holes to make me wonder if he was Swiss. His eyes were dead, but seeing that he was a vampire, that wasn't surprising. This was a different level of dead, though. It was the kind of dead that even vampires couldn't transcend.

And that's when he started losing his size, returning slowly back to his original state.

Another suit.

Jasmine reached into his pocket and pulled out his ID. She stepped away and called it in.

I could only imagine the bruising that a normal would have suffered at the hands of the two ubernaturals we'd

JOHN P. LOGSDON & CHRISTOPHER P. YOUNG

faced tonight. If it weren't for my ability to heal so quickly, I would be looking at a solid month of recovery. A couple hours of rest would be good enough to get me back on track again.

"Lydia says this guy is one of the main players in the finance department here at the Nugget," Jasmine announced.

"Hmmm," I said, gently pushing myself back to my feet. I shook my head to clear the mental fog. "So we've got two finance types from two casinos turning into a big bad wolf and a naughty vampire. Coincidence?"

"Never seen anything like it," Rachel said. "We've been walking this beat for a long time. This is a first."

"Lydia," I said through the connector, *"are there any records about supernaturals getting this powerful in the past?"*

"Accessing, honey," she said. *"Nothing listed in the primary records, no. There have been a number of collaborative power plays over the years, but nothing recent. Even then, it was groups, not individuals."*

"Anything on the non-primary records?" asked Rachel.

"I only have access to primary records," Lydia replied studiously.

"Thanks, Lydia," I said. *"If you could let The Spin know that we're finished here, that'd be super."*

"You got it, sugar. I'll also tell the finance department at the Nugget what's going on, so they don't expect this particular executive in the office tomorrow."

CHAPTER 9

*B*y the time we arrived back at base, I'd received word that my Aston Martin was towed in by our clean-up crew. They'd have the window replaced in no time and a new set of tires in place, balanced, and shined. I never understood why Felicia refused to use their services on her Camaro, but I assumed it had to do with her desire to be an automotive purist. She wanted authentic parts.

I followed behind Jasmine as she pushed through the main door to the PPD.

The configuration of the interior was interesting. It ran a semi-circle that allowed everyone to have their own windowed office. Stairs went up on the left and right, landing on a walkway that led to each office. Under the offices sat a conference room, a small break room, temporary holding cells, the access area to the clean-up crew's section, and the engineering bay. That's where Lydia was housed, which was also the office of our resident hardware and software hacker, a pixie by the name of Turbo.

"Welcome back, honey," Lydia said as I climbed the stairs to the second level. *"The Directors want to see you."*

"Figured they might."

The Directors were members of the various factions in Vegas. They didn't represent all of the supernatural races, but they covered the most dominant ones in Vegas. Other cities, like New York and London, had additional Directors added to the ones we got.

"Keep your ears open for us, Lydia," I said as I stepped into my office, speaking aloud. "I have a feeling we're going to have more trouble with this new kind of monster."

"Of course, love," she answered through one of the speakers in the room.

Where some chose simple over extravagant, I was one of those who enjoyed the good life. Hence the Aston Martin. People like Rachel had a flat desk with a basic office chair. I opted for a crescent mahogany with the high-back leather. It wasn't a power play; it was just that I liked nice things. Nice suits, nice cars, nice desks, and so on.

The department didn't buy any of it for me. That would be a misappropriation of funds. I used the money from the trust fund my parents had set up for me. They'd died in a plane crash when I was two. I never really knew them, though now and then the blur of a face would pass my memories. There were no relatives either. I'd been left at two years old with a bundle of cash that would ripen by the time I'd reached 18. That meant a life of foster homes. Since I didn't change forms like a vampire or a werewolf, and since I didn't go around casting spells when I got irritable, the state assumed I was just your average, everyday normal. I got placed with multiple families over the years, but it never worked out because my abilities far exceeded the average parent's capability to contain me. By the time the state figured out that I was something different, I was already in my late teens. So they took me out of the normals' system, studied me a fair bit, stuck me into an immersion program with supernaturals, and taught me the ins and outs of how to be a cop. When my trust fund hit, I figured the universe owed me one and thus began my indulgence with the finer things. I blew a lot of cash in the first couple of years, but soon got a finance manager to help me take care of it so I wouldn't have to wait for early retirement, should the desire ever come.

And as I looked at the door sitting in the back of my office, I started thinking that now would be a good time to retire.

"Going in," I announced to Lydia. "Lock down my office, please."

"Have fun, sweetie," she said moments before the clanking sound of locks closed my office and the windows darkened.

"Sure."

I opened the door and stepped into a room that was probably only the size of a closet, but it felt much larger. It was a connectivity portal that allowed the Directors to engage in questioning while never leaving the confines of their own offices.

There were four of them seated in congressional-hearing fashion, all facing me while I was relegated to taking the chair of the guy being questioned.

Typically these were only done every couple of weeks as standard protocol, but whenever something interesting happened, they were more frequent. Seeing as how we'd just dealt with two ubernaturals, I completely expected they'd be anxious to learn what the hell was going on.

Silver, the head of the Vegas Vampire Coalition (VVC) sat on the far left. He was the lurker of the bunch. Quiet, but poignant.

Next was Zack, the current point of contact for the Vegas Werewolf Pack. He'd held the position longer than most. Probably because he wasn't the type who would back down from a fight. Doggies were very hierarchical, after all.

O was the leader of the Vegas Crimson Focus Mages. They were a group considered to be of the more powerful magical class in the world, not just Vegas. All three mages in my little PPD division belonged to his club.

Last was EQK, who represented the Vegas Pixies. He often snickered and giggled during the meetings, and he would sometimes say things that seemed inappropriate at best.

While I could make out certain features of each, their faces vanished from memory the moment they entered my psyche. It had something to do with the need for secrecy. I'm sure they could spot me on the street, but I wouldn't even be able to identify any of them in a lineup.

"Let's get started," said O, followed immediately by a giggle from EQK. "Mr. Dex, we have been informed about two strange occurrences in the area. One involving a werewolf and the other a vampire."

"That's correct, sir," I said.

"What have you learned of them?"

"Nothing yet," I answered. "I just know that both were far more powerful than anything I've ever encountered as a cop."

"What was different?" asked Zack.

I leaned back and crossed my legs. "Well, they were huge, for one. Very strong." I tapped my finger on my knee. "And they were immune to normal effects. Silver breakers did nothing against the werewolf and woods didn't stop the vampire."

"I heard you shot one in the cock," said EQK with an uncontrollable giggle.

"I was aiming for his abdomen, sir," I lied, but tried to keep a professional visage. "He was just taller than I'd expected."

"Was it really necessary to kill them?" asked Silver in a dark voice.

"Yes, sir. They were tearing things up and acting all sorts of naughty. If we didn't take them down, there would have been a lot of normals affected."

"Seems there already were," O stated. "The Spin is working on cleaning things up, but this is a tough assignment for them."

"I'd imagine so," I agreed. "We did the best we could with the knowledge we had, sir."

"I'm sure you did," said O genuinely. "That will be all

for now. Keep us posted regarding your investigation, Mr. Dex."

"Most definitely, sir."

CHAPTER 10

The crew gathered in the conference room. We were joined by one of our gurus, Warren Lloyd.

Warren was a wizard who specialized in runes and grandiose spells. He looked a bit like a hippie. Not so much like a Gandalf or anything, but more like a laid-back surfer dude who'd spent a little too much time in the sun during his younger years.

"Got anything yet?" I asked the room as I took the chair at the head of the table.

"Well," started Griff, "we were already aware that the werewolf and vampire were both executives in finance, so we made a couple of calls to see if their bosses might have noticed anything strange."

"And?"

"First, they were more than irritated that we were calling in the middle of the night. Once they realized what had occurred, they were more than cooperative." Griff looked down at his iPad. "Richard Brenkin's manager stated that Richard had taken off a little early in the day to attend a finance seminar on the old strip. Bill Preston..."

"The vampire?" I asked, interrupting.

"Indeed," said Griff. "His superior said the same thing about him."

"Interesting. So, both of them leave work around the same time, head down to a seminar in Old Town, and end up turning into crazed versions of themselves with powers far beyond their norm." I sniffed. "Some seminar."

"Seems so," agreed Jasmine.

"Were there any records as to precisely where this seminar was being held?"

"Their managers did not possess that information, I'm afraid," Griff replied. "It appears that executives are attending so many of these events on a monthly basis that they neglect to keep tabs on all of it."

That made little sense to me, but we were talking about companies who had so much money funneling through on a daily basis that they didn't likely care about where it was all being spent. There was probably somebody tasked with keeping receipts, but it wouldn't be the brass.

"My worry is that we're going to see more of this soon," I said while scratching at the table. "I highly doubt that only two people attended a finance seminar, after all."

"Good point," said Rachel, seemingly on the mend regarding our earlier tiff. I hoped, anyway. "We need to find out where the seminar was held and get a list of attendees."

"Agreed." I turned to our specialist. "Warren, have you

something to add to this discussion or are you just listening in?"

He cleared his throat and shifted in his seat a bit.

While he was more chill than most people in the PPD, he was also a bit shy, and he wasn't gifted with what you'd call grace under pressure.

"I was going over the information that you guys brought in," he answered in a somewhat nerdy voice, "and I have a few questions so I can dig deeper."

I nodded at him. "Go on."

"You said that the werewolf was a fast swimmer, right?"

"Incredibly," I replied. "His dog paddle was very impressive."

"And he drove your car while in wolf form?"

Rachel's attitude returned at the mention of Fido driving her around in my car. I fought to ignore it.

"Like a pro."

"Okay," said Warren, jotting down notes the entire time. "The vampire was calling out to his minions, right?"

"Yeah," answered Chuck. "He looked like a preacher up on a pulpit. It was kind of freaky."

"And he didn't attack you straightaway like the werewolf did, correct?"

"He held his resolve until Charles engaged," Griff said, using Chuck's formal name. "Once we backed off, the vampire went about throwing things again before climbing onto the roof. After that, he ignored us entirely, until the Chief filled his nethers with lead, that is."

"Wood," I amended.

"Fine, you shot him in the wood…"

"No, I mean that I used wood breakers, and he looked like he was about to rip me in two, thank you very much."

Warren was nodding his head and chewing his lip. It appeared that he was on to something, but he had a tendency of keeping quiet until he was certain. Still, I'd push him where I could.

"Does this sound familiar or something, Warren?"

"Huh?" He looked up as if being shaken from a dream. "Oh, I'm not sure. I'll have to do some study. There are records in the archives that I swear said something about…"

"Sorry to interrupt, puddin'," Lydia announced through the room's speakers, "but we have reports of a fae attacking other supernaturals down at the Wynn."

"Dammit." I was hoping to get some decent insight on Warren's thoughts. "Everybody get rolling," I commanded. "Warren, keep after this…well, whatever it is you're after. We need answers yesterday."

"I'll have to see this creature firsthand," he said, standing up with the rest of us.

I hesitated. Warren was good at his job, but he was slow. All wizards were slow. They had to think and plan… and use a wand. I didn't have time to babysit and I wasn't about to risk any of my agents having to do it either.

"It's too dangerous," I started, but then stopped when I caught sight of Serena Buchanan, our resident forensics expert. She was standing at the vending machine in our meager break room.

Serena was one of those vampires who could have played the part of a succubus. Actually, she *had* played that part a couple of times with me in the past, and she was better at it than an actual succubus I'd once dated. And she was gifted with an hourglass figure that made you want to study the mysteries of time.

"Get Serena to bring you," I said to Warren as I fought to keep my mind on business, "but stay out of the way until we've subdued this fae, got it?"

"Got it."

CHAPTER 11

*F*ae were known to be decent and helpful, even though they loved playing practical jokes and just being generally tricky. Like humans, they came in all shapes and sizes, though they most often looked like an incredibly attractive normal.

This thing did *not* look like an average fae.

Similar to the anomalies we faced earlier, she was tall, broad shouldered, and muscular. But instead of the typical great looks, she was rather hideous. Her face was contorted into a deep sneer, her eyes were yellow, and there were scars and scales running haphazardly down the sides of her exposed neck.

The main casino floor was awash with fallen bodies. They were all supernaturals, just as the report said, and they were writhing about, signaling that they hadn't been killed... yet.

A mass of normals were standing around the periphery with mixed looks of fascination and terror.

Great.

"Split up," I commanded as the fae took notice.

"Oh, look," she said, pointing a long-nailed finger directly at me. "Members of the famous Las Vegas Paranormal Police Department have been sent to stop me." She bowed at the waist and swung her head around from side to side, causing the normals to cringe in fear. "Isn't that exciting?"

Nobody said a word as my crew and I kept moving forward.

"Do you think I should just give up or should I resist?" she called to the crowd.

"Resist, baby!" I looked over at the drunk normal who was yelling in a slurred way. He was holding up a glass of something. "Woohoo!"

A number of other normals cheered along with the guy, obviously stepping to the side of the fence that tried to convince them this was naught but a show.

The fae laughed heartily and then turned back to look at me. She shrugged. "Sorry, baby, but the people have spoken."

"Collateral damage is only going to make this worse on you," I called back, keeping my pace steady but easy.

"Oh no," she said, clutching her chest, "we wouldn't want that, now would we?"

Why was it that supernaturals who were up to no good felt compelled to make a show of it? I mean, not all of them did. The vampire who'd been torn apart by Fido was at least somewhat discreet with his attack on the normal. But whenever a super decided they were gonna go out big, they really jumped in ass-first.

"Rachel," I said out of the corner of my mouth, "can you give this thing a taste of fire for me, please?"

"With pleasure," Rachel replied, releasing a ball of energy moments later.

The fae held up a hand and caught the ball. She looked it over for a moment, spinning it around like it was some sort of plaything, and then flung it back with force.

"Shit," said Rachel as she dived out of the way.

The energy ball smashed into a craps table, demolishing it instantly. Fortunately it had been devoid of gamblers, but the dealer who'd been waiting for customers hadn't been so lucky. He was knocked off his feet, flying across the room until he crunched into a wall with a sickening thud. A smear of blood oozed behind him as he slid down with lifeless eyes.

"Oops," said the fae while blinking innocently.

It was silent for a second until the drunk normal yelled "Woohoo!" again. That elicited another round of cheers from the rest of the crowd.

Damn sheep.

"I think they like me," the fae said, smiling in such a way that made her look even more grotesque. "They really, really like me!"

"Unload on this bitch," I yelled and then emptied my gun at her.

To her credit, she blocked a lot of the shots with magic, but we were sending far too much for her to contain.

It seemed that each one of these beasties was getting tougher than the last. Fido hadn't been too difficult to manage. Captain Vampire had given Griff and Chuck a hard time, but he was taken out pretty easily after I neutered him. That thought made me pause and think how it was almost a shame I hadn't shot Fido in the sunless region instead of Captain Vampire. The neutered line would have made for humorous conversation at the Paranormal Policeman's Ball.

But now we were faced with a fae who was actually *blocking* our attempts to take her out.

This was dicey.

She plunged into one of the concierge stations as the customer service agents jumped out, screaming.

The normals laughed at this and started to boo us.

"Seriously?" said Rachel, giving me a 'what-the-fuck' look in the process.

I shrugged at her.

The normals had no idea what was going on. For all they knew, this was a new Vegas show that was exclusive to the Wynn. The number of times The Spin had used that little explanation for all the mishaps over the years made it the obvious go-to rationalization for a normal. Frankly, it was for the best that they felt this way, but it *did* make those of us at the PPD feel like we were the bad guys from time to time.

"*Puddin',*" Lydia said through the connector as I changed out my mag, "*you're not going to believe this, but we have a rogue wizard sticking runes in all of the bathrooms where you are.*"

"You're kidding," I said as I motioned the crew to shred the customer service station. "*Is it one of these big-bad types?*"

58

"*I don't think so, lover,*" she answered. "*He's just being a pain in the patootie. Quite literally, from what I understand.*"

Energy and bullets connected with the customer service station, blowing fragments of wood up into the air.

Griff put up a containment wall around the normals so they wouldn't get impacted with shrapnel, but a number of splinters threatened to penetrate my back as I turned away and crouched.

One piece shot cleanly through my earlobe.

I'd always wanted to try a piercing, just not like this.

The fae jumped straight up and cast her own spell of protection. Jasmine's next blast hit with enough force to smack the creepy creature into the ceiling, but she landed gracefully as the shockwave of her spell blew my team off their feet.

"This is fun," the fae yelled out. "Betcha can't catch me!"

With that, she spun on her heel and took off through the casino.

CHAPTER 12

I'd told Lydia to put Warren and Serena on the wizard who was playing bathroom pranks. It was likely just some kid who had finally learned enough about spell casting to be annoying. But it was the PPD's responsibility to take care of these things, stupid or not.

"*You might want to get Paula down here,*" I called out to Lydia as we chased the massive fae through the casino. "*I think this is going to take her some time to sort out.*"

"*She's already been notified, sweetie.*"

"*Great,*" I said, jumping a table the fae had flipped over in her wake. "*Also, I think we're going to need our clean-up crew on this one. There's a lot of damage to the casino.*"

"*Sending them along.*"

The fae took to the spiral staircase, bolting up the stairs faster than anyone should be capable of going.

I held up my hand to stop my crew.

"Griff and Chuck," I said while fighting to catch my breath, "hit the back way so we're not all approaching from the same side."

They nodded and took off.

"Felicia, take Jasmine and get that security guard over there to take you through the supernaturals' area."

That left me, Rachel, and a bunch of swaggering drunks who were calling us various names.

"I'm guessing we're going to be following that thing directly?" Rachel more said than asked.

I nodded. "Unless you have a better plan?"

"Run in the opposite direction?" she suggested.

"As if you would." I laughed and then looked up the stairs as a few shrieks sounded.

Obviously, our lovely fae was still having fun.

"True," Rachel replied an instant before she hit the steps.

I sped along after her, my legs burning from climbing at breakneck speed.

We got to the top and looked around. The furniture was all intact and there weren't any bodies on the floor.

"Where'd she go?" I asked rhetorically.

"Over here, assholes," the fae cackled and launched a stream of wind at us, knocking Rachel into me and crashing us both to the ground.

Rachel had spun before we smashed together, meaning that I was lying on my back and she was on top of me, face to face.

"Ah, the memories," I said as she frowned and pushed herself back up. "What?" I called after her while getting to my feet and chasing her down the corridor. "Don't hide from your feelings, Rachel."

She held up a single finger in response before cutting a corner.

Just as I was about to hit the corner myself, I heard another cackle and watched Rachel's body fly through the air.

I dived forward a moment later and fired down at the fae before my shoulder slammed into the far wall.

"Dammit," the fae yelled, signaling at least one of my bullets had struck. It wouldn't stop her, but it had to hurt. "You fucker," she said as she turned and unleashed a wave of kinetic energy my way.

I'd be remiss if I didn't explain how much it hurts to be wrapped in a ball of electric joy. Imagine having your balls sliced open and dipped in lemon juice while someone holds smelling salts under your nose to ensure you can't pass out from the pain. Now, I realize that this point of reference may not be fitting for everyone, so let's just say that the misery radiating through my body was more intense than having a needle stuck in your taint (and everyone has a taint). But the needle doesn't stay still. It gets twisted around this way and that as you wriggle and scream. Of course, if you're a masochist this may actually be pleasurable for you in some odd way. But being that I'm *not* a masochist, the pain I was enduring was far less than enjoyable.

When the energy finally dissipated, the only word I could mutter was a shivered "fuck."

"You can say that again," Rachel agreed, dragging me to my feet. "I'm starting to think that getting a Desert Eagle may not be such a bad idea after all."

"Yes," I concurred, fighting to regain control of my body. "Besides, we *are* in the desert, so…"

"Yeah, right."

A mass of people poured out of the room that the fae had gone into, and they looked to be running for their lives.

Thankfully, it was a supernaturals area.

Every hotel had one.

Normals weren't allowed in, unless they were specifically invited, were on the executive team, or were acting in the role of servant. Any unauthorized normal who tried to enter would sound off an alarm, which would result in them having their memory rewritten to think that they'd accidentally walked into one of the many offices littering each casino on the upper levels. It's not all fun and games working in Vegas, you know.

"Looks like she's playing again," Rachel said, running toward the source of the pain in direct contrast with the others who were trying to get away.

"Yes," I said, wincing with each step. "Let's run toward her. That's a great plan."

CHAPTER 13

My body was still hating life as the last of the people left the room that contained the giddy fae. That she remained so sinisterly cheerful was a testament to how warped she was. I could only guess that my gunshot hadn't fully connected.

Rachel jumped to the other side of the entrance and glanced around, and then shook her head. I did a quick survey of the area and found nothing either.

"Window?" I asked, but Rachel merely shrugged in response. "Who knew that fae-hunting could be such a hoot."

"Yep."

"Cover me," I said as I launched into the room, rolled once, and came up into a crouched position. My equilibrium wasn't at full yet, so I overshot the landing a little and bumped into a wastebasket that fell over in response.

"Idiot," said Rachel before rolling in the opposite direction, coming up expertly with hands aglow.

"Sorry that some of us are deemed more dangerous than others," I retaliated, regaining my footing. "Maybe if you were as threatening as me, you'd get the energy spells thrown in your face instead of the simple wind ones."

Rachel glanced in my general direction. "Keep talking, flyboy, and I'll give you an energy spell you'll not soon forget."

"Promises, promises," I said while continuing to scan the room. "She's not here."

"Or she's hidden."

"Right," I said, standing up but keeping my gun at the ready. "A seven-foot chick who looks like a wrestler is hiding in the middle of a mostly open room."

"You're a seven-foot chick who looks like a wrestler," Rachel snarked while slinking down the side wall.

"Real mature."

I'd gotten over to the curtains and started kicking at them, when Jasmine spoke through the connector.

"*Chief,*" she said, "*it looks like the fae is scaling the outer wall.*"

We threw back the heavy curtains to find none of the windows were broken, and it wasn't like they could be opened either. Most of these buildings were made so people couldn't easily jump should the pressure get too much for them.

"*Well, that's a mystery,*" I said both to Rachel and through the connector. "*How the hell did she get outside?*"

"*Morphing spell,*" Rachel answered.

"*Yep,*" agreed Jasmine. "*Fae do morph when they want to.*"

"*I'm well aware of that,*" I replied. "*I took all the same courses you guys did. My point is that all the windows in here are intact, so what exactly could she have morphed into that would allow...*" And that's when I looked up and saw that a grate on the ventilation shaft had been torn off. "*A mouse or a rat,*" I said, pointing.

"*Terrific,*" said Rachel. "*So how the hell are we supposed to get her off the side of a building?*"

"*I don't suppose we have any dragons in the area who are willing to give us a hand?*"

"*None registered,*" Jasmine stated. "*It was the first thing I had Lydia check when we saw the fae climbing around outside. There haven't been any topside in a very long time, though. Last one was back before the Old War.*"

I stuck my gun back in its holster and started back out the way we'd come in. People were asking questions but I held them off, explaining that we were still trying to catch the damn fae and didn't have time for chitchat. They didn't look pleased with that answer, but my first priority was apprehending the bad guys, not managing customer support.

"*Do you still have eyes on this thing?*" I asked as we took the spiral staircase back down to the main floor.

"*Yes,*" Jasmine answered. "*She's almost around the back of the building. Should be at ground level pretty soon.*"

"*Good. Everyone get down to the back area and unleash everything you've got into this damn fae's head. I want her stopped before she can fire off any more of those blasted energy spells.*"

"*On our way,*" both teams replied.

"*Lydia, requisition me a Desert Eagle immediately, and get Turbo to build me bullets for it.*"

"*You got it, baby,*" she said in a sweet voice that was in

complete conflict with the fact that I'd just ordered a weapon meant for mayhem. *"Did you want the forty-four caliber or the fifty?"*

"Get him the fifty," Rachel answered for me. *"And get me one, too, while you're at it."*

"I shall comply, Miss Cress," affirmed Lydia, without the same tenderness she gave to me.

"Ugh," Rachel said as we exited the back of the building.

I ignored the irritation in my partner's voice.

Was it my fault that everyone treated Lydia like a computer instead of like a person? No. They acted like she was nothing but an informational tool, and so that's how she replied to them. I used her for intel too, obviously, but I would occasionally throw in a personal gem to let her know that she was more than that to me. She was a member of my team. Besides, maybe someday she'd be integrated into a super-hot android body and I'd be the recipient of much affection.

"I know what you're thinking," Rachel said with a glare. "You're a freak, you know that?"

"You have no idea," I replied, grinning.

"Sadly, I do."

The fae dropped down onto the street and took a look around, spotting us and exhaling hard. She began backing away while squinting. It wasn't a pretty sight.

"You just don't give up, do you?" she said as she formed another round of energy in her hands.

"Wait!" I called out, holding up my gun as a thought hit me.

"What are you doing?" Rachel whispered.

"Buying us time for the others to get here. I hope."

The fae tilted her head but kept the energy flowing between her hands. It was clear that she was curious as to why I was holding my hands up in surrender, but she was obviously not stupid.

"I probably shouldn't tell you this," she said in a helpful tone of voice, "but you'd be smarter to have your gun pointed at me. At least you'd have a chance that way."

"That's exactly why I'm not pointing it at you," I replied while taking things a step further and setting the gun on the ground. "It's clear that we can't defeat you. You're just more powerful than the werewolf and the vampire we faced earlier."

"That's true." She kept the energy rolling. Then she nodded toward Rachel. "What about your wizard pal over there?"

"Mage," Rachel corrected, her eye twitching.

"What?" asked the fae.

"I'm a mage, not a wizard."

"So?"

"Just ignore the mage, baby," I said, hoping that the fae would be even more confused if I hit on her. "She's no match for you anyway."

The fae raised an eyebrow. "Baby?"

"What can I say?" I said with a shrug. "There's something about a"—this was difficult—"rambunctious fae with the ability to do energy blasts that gets my motor running."

"Seriously?"

"Yeah," agreed Rachel, "seriously?"

"Of course," I answered, turning briefly to give Rachel the stink-eye. "Power is intoxicating."

"Right," said the fae. She then cleared her throat. "I'm flattered and all. I *truly* am. But I think you're missing a few things."

"Like what, my princess?" I said, batting my eyelashes as best I could.

"One, I'm not into dudes." She cracked her neck from side to side. "Two, I don't dig vampires. And, three, you can't trick a trickster."

With that, she unleashed another ball of energy right at my chest as I yelled out, "I'm not a fucking vampire!"

CHAPTER 14

$\mathcal{M}$imicking the fae's list of three, the following things happened at that moment.

The first was me crying like a baby as the energy pulsed through my body, threatening to fry me from the inside out; the second was that my hand landed serendipitously on my gun as I hit the ground; and the third was that the rest of my crew jumped out into the clearing and began firing like mad at the damned fae.

"Give her everything we've got," commanded Rachel.

All hell was breaking loose as projectiles ripped through the beastie. Fireballs smacked against her chest and ice shards pattered her legs. She was catching and throwing back what she could, but Griff had apparently put up a one-way shield to hold off her attempts at retaliation.

"Tar...tar..." I tried yelling but I couldn't stop convulsing.

"What?" said Rachel.

"Her...hea...head," I yelled. "Shoo..."

"Aim everything at her head," Rachel called out, finally catching on to what I was trying to say.

I got only one shot off myself before my brain could no longer manage the exquisite pain I was experiencing.

The gun fell from my hand and I blacked out for a second.

Light came in one moment and went dark the next as my consciousness was fading in and out. I wanted it to leave my brain's power in the off position until the energy of the fae's spell had run its course, but that was one of the problems with being a fast healer—without some pretty heavy sedatives, you got to enjoy the agony of healing in real-time.

During one of my awake moments, I saw the fae drop to one knee. She was clearly being overwhelmed. There was only so much damage a head could take, after all.

I struggled to grab my gun again, but my hands just wouldn't cooperate.

That's when a black leather boot stepped next to my head and a stark-white hand reached down to grab the weapon. Shots rang out, catching the fae from another angle, dropping her into finality.

I rolled onto my back, shuddering.

Standing above me was Serena.

She was holding my gun with a malevolent look on her face. This wasn't the first time I'd seen her like this, gun and all. As I recall, I had been in a fair bit of pain back then, too...the exquisite kind.

I grinned as she looked down at me and winked.

"She d...d...dead?"

"Most definitely," Serena answered, kneeling to help me to sit up. Once I was propped against her, she said, "Stay still."

Her hands were magic, in more ways than one. While she wasn't a spell-caster, she had the ability to dissipate the effects of spells in rapid fashion. It only took a couple more seconds before the agony dispersed and I was left feeling the general ache of having been encased in electricity.

"Thank you," I said genuinely. "That wasn't as much fun as it appeared."

"You should have used your safe word," Serena said with a wink as she helped me up.

"She knows about your safe word?" said Rachel, shaking her head.

"One of them," I replied with a weak smile. Then I turned to Warren. "Did you catch the bathroom bandit?"

"Yes," he said. "Just a kid playing pranks. I told him to undo everything immediately or he'd be looking at jail time. He's working on it."

"Hopefully it wasn't anything too bad," I said, not really caring all that much.

"Backward flushing toilets, itching toilet paper, splash shields…" Warren said and then stared across at the fallen fae while slowly turning green. "That's disgusting."

Then he puked all over my shoes.

CHAPTER 15

I'd fully recovered from the fae's energy blast and had used an outside faucet to rinse Warren's dinner off my shoes. He had gotten control of himself and was busily studying the dead monster, when Paula Rose stepped out of the building, calling my name.

"Shit," I whispered as Serena raised an eyebrow at me and wisely walked away.

Paula did not look pleased as she approached.

"Paula?" I said, acting surprised. "What brings you here?"

"Funny," she said. "Do you have any idea how I'm supposed to manage this fine mess you've gotten me into?"

"First off," I replied, pointing at the fallen fae, "that's who you should be yelling at, not me. We weren't the ones running around and causing all sorts of destruction. Mostly. In fact, I *personally* only fired off a couple of rounds."

Her eye was twitching. "Was that before or after the

customer service desk in the center of the casino was blown to shit?"

"Forgot about that." I coughed and my ribs pulsed. "Okay, so we had a little bit to do with the light show, but we wouldn't have been here at all had it not been for that thing."

It was clear that Paula was fighting to maintain her cool. I couldn't say that I blamed her, either. Not that it was *my* fault this all came down, but having to constantly cover our asses couldn't have been the funnest of jobs. No doubt it was better than working in something like, say, retail. But then again, what wasn't?

"Just say it's another—"

"Another show?" she interrupted, glaring at me. "How many times am I going to use that lame excuse before people start getting wise to the bullshit?"

"We *are* in Vegas," I pointed out. "You can probably use that one for a good long time. Already have, actually."

"Making me a joke among my peers," she scoffed.

"You have peers?" I asked, instantly regretting it.

Her hand was firmly placed on her hip now. "You son of a bitch. Do you have any idea how hard my job is?"

"I'm guessing it's better than working in retail…"

"I barely ever get any sleep, and even when I do it's broken up with a constant barrage of dreams involving me trying to figure out clever ways to cover the mayhem that you and your team cause every week." She kicked a rock that was lying on the street, sending it flying to the curb. "I have zero social life, most of my employees are idiots, and I'm not a supernatural."

"I thought you were pretty decent when we…" I

stopped. Now, apparently, was not the time for levity. "Sorry."

She sighed. "Do you think it's remotely possible for you and your gang of misfits—"

"I think you mean police officers."

"I know what I mean, thank you very much." Her foot was tapping now. "Do you think you can maybe just stop blowing up stuff for the rest of the night?"

I wanted to say that we could, but it wasn't like I had any control over any of this. The monsters that kept showing up weren't exactly invited, after all.

"I can't promise that," I answered, "but I could sure as hell go for a few hours of peace and quiet myself."

At that admission, she dropped the hand off her hip and quit tapping her foot. It was obvious she was as tired as I felt, and the fact that she was a normal made it even tougher on her. What she needed was a nice back rub, but I knew better than to make the offer right now. Most of the women standing here already thought I was the biggest pig on the planet. Except for Serena, of course, who rather approved of my playful lifestyle.

"Look," I said more carefully, "we'll do what we can to minimize destruction for a while. Just hope that no more of these beasties show up. Maybe that 'bad things always happen in threes' superstition will ring true tonight."

"I hope so," she said and then walked back into the building.

"Chief," Warren said, helping to take my mind off Paula's intoxicating form, "we've got bigger problems than we thought."

"Of course we do."

CHAPTER 16

Warren was going through his iPad, sharing the details of multiple runes spells with Serena while the rest of us milled around, waiting for the next bad thing to show up.

The fae had been one Helen Guthrie who, not surprisingly, worked in the finance department of the Wynn. She appeared to be in her late seventies. She had gray hair, steel-rimmed glasses, and a tweed jacket.

A white van approached and the familiar face of Rick Portman stepped out. He was the coroner for the supernatural community. We brought him a fair amount of business. Portman was one of the few werebears in Vegas. He was a good guy, too. Never gave me crap about his team having to do clean-up.

"How's it hanging, Dex?" he said while gripping my hand firmly.

Not very many people called me solely by my last name. It was kind of a pet peeve of mine. But Portman was different. He did it in a way that wasn't condescending. It was just how he spoke.

"To the left," I replied. "You?"

"Living the dream, as they say." He glanced around and saw the body. "Killing little old ladies now, eh?"

"You should have seen her twenty minutes ago. Not only was she a fair bit bigger, she was also *not* what you'd consider grandmother material."

"Hmmm." He walked over and knelt down beside Warren. "Took off half her head. Nice."

"Don't remind me," Warren begged.

"Yeah, don't," I agreed. "He's already done the technicolor yawn on my shoes once."

Portman nodded and stood back up. He'd obviously seen a lot of things like this in his life because he looked completely desensitized. Through all the years of being a cop, I never got used to it.

"Gonna be long?" Portman said, glancing at his watch. "If so, I'll head in for a quick game of blackjack."

"Almost done," Warren answered, drawing another design on the ground by the body. "You all may want to stand back. I'm not sure if I'm right or not, but you don't want to be too close if I am."

"What are you right about, again?" I asked before he could activate the runes.

"I think we're dealing with demons," he replied.

"Oooh," said Portman with renewed interest.

I stepped over to stand beside Warren.

"Now, I'm no expert when it comes to dealing with demons, but if that *does* turn out to be one, what kind of plan do you have in place to contain it?"

Warren glanced at me. "I hadn't thought of that."

"Might be a good idea, no?"

"Definitely," he agreed with a nod. "Can I borrow the mages?"

This happened with Warren from time to time. He wouldn't think things through all the way, and then when it got pointed out, he would forget how things worked.

"We're on the same team, Warren," I said, patting him on the shoulder. "There's no borrowing, just tell them what you need."

He went about giving instructions as I turned my attention back to Portman.

"This will probably take a few minutes, if you'd rather come back."

"And miss a shot at seeing a demon?" he said incredulously. "Not a chance, Dex. I'll stay a few."

There weren't any specific metals or fibers that I knew of for shooting at demons, but seeing as I only had wood and silver breakers on hand, it wouldn't have mattered anyway. Fortunately, we had three mages and a wizard all set and ready to combat whatever came out of the little old lady, assuming Warren was right.

"Everyone ready?"

They all nodded. I pulled up my gun and looked down the sights, aiming it squarely at what remained of Helen's head.

Warren waved his hands around and chanted something in a language that sounded made up. I knew it was for real because I'd heard it many times over the years, but I had to admit that I always cracked a smile when hearing it. Imagine a bunch of tone-deaf pygmies trying to sing the theme song from *Saturday Night Fever* and you'll get the general idea.

The runes began glowing, each with its own variety of colors. They pulsed in rhythm with Warren's chants. Some were brighter than others at first, but soon they fell into sequence and the ground trembled slightly.

There was a smell that permeated the air moments later. Lilies mixed with a zoo and a bucket of week-old fish came to mind. It wasn't exactly pleasant.

"Damn, Dex," Portman said, taking a step away.

"It wasn't me," I shot back while nodding at Warren and the fallen accountant.

"Oh right, sorry."

A crackling sound rang out and the body began to shift.

Helen's chest heaved a few times.

Then she convulsed and began an uncontrolled dance where she slapped the ground and kicked her feet, rolling violently from side to side.

"What's happening?" I asked, tightening my grip on the gun.

"I think we're going to find out if our resident wizard is right or not," Chuck answered as Warren continued his chanting.

Jasmine, Rachel, and Griff had their hands linked. They were in a deep meditative state, which they sometimes did when they were trying to rebuild their power after a lengthy battle. They also said they'd practiced this technique together, just in case even bigger spells were ever needed. I was hoping they wouldn't be needed now, but I was damn glad they'd practiced.

A low moan came from the body of Helen Guthrie after the flopping stopped. It slowly increased in volume as multicolored snowflakes fell on her, each pulsing momentarily before bursting into flames.

An eerily distant scream spilled from her lips and then stopped abruptly.

Her only available eye snapped open.

"Shit," said Portman, jumping backward. "Didn't see that coming."

I barely held my ground, truth be told.

The eye was blood red with a thin yellow iris. It looked as lifeless as the rest of her body for a second, then it started moving, studying each face in my crew before stopping on me.

CHAPTER 17

I gulped as I studied that eye. It held a level of accusation that wasn't exactly giving me the warm and fuzzies. Did it know I was the leader of this crew or something? Captain Vampire knew, but he was one to watch the supernatural news a lot.

"So it's looking at me for some reason," I said to Warren. "Any idea why that might be?"

"Not a clue."

"Maybe you slept with it, too?" Rachel suggested as the three mages separated and cast a spell that enveloped the creature.

"I've never slept with a demon," I shot back. Then I frowned and chewed my lip. "At least I don't think I have."

"You are the one who is like none other," the gurgling voice of Helen Guthrie said.

My eyebrows went up. "Maybe I *did* sleep with it."

I wasn't sure if I was supposed to feel fear or flattery.

"You are the amalgamite."

Fear, then.

I took another step back while keeping my gun up. It wasn't likely to do much against a demon, but you never know until you try. Maybe there were holy water breaker bullets somewhere out there?

"Speak!" it demanded.

"Uh," I said with a concerned look. "Yeah, okay, so I'm the amalgamite. So what? Is that a crime?"

"Yes," hissed the demon.

"Oh. Well, shit."

"Yours is an invalid soul."

Rachel snorted. "He's kind of a dick, too."

"Hey!"

The demon moved to get up, but the mages all channeled together and drove massive amounts of energy into it, keeping it pressed to the ground. It pushed against them and seemed to be doing a decent job of fighting back.

"We can't hold this forever, Warren," Jasmine said through clenched teeth. "I'm assuming you have something ready?"

"Almost," he replied, studying his device again.

"What the hell, Warren?" I said, unable to tear my eyes away from the demon. "Wasn't I clear when I said we needed to have a plan for this thing?"

"I did," Warren retaliated with a shriek. "They're keeping him in check while I study."

I glanced at him for a second and then back at the demon.

"That's not a plan. That's a plan to make a plan."

"Allow him to focus on the task at hand, please," Griff

stated in his ever-calm voice. "This is rather trying on our power reserves."

It was all I could do to keep my mouth shut. One thing was for sure, Warren and I were going to have a little talk about the virtues of proper planning. First I'd have to create a plan for that talk, but it'd happen... eventually.

"Amalgamite," hissed the demon, "why were you allowed to live?"

The only thing worse than being called by my last name was being called "amalgamite."

It was just rude.

"First off, my name is Ian Dex," I said in irritated fashion. "Secondly, nobody knew of my situation until I was older."

"And yet you're still alive," it noted.

"Are all demons as quick on the uptake as you?" I asked with an edge.

It tried to get up again. The power of its push staggered my mages. They all gave me dirty looks.

"Again," Rachel groaned as the sweat poured off her brow, "pissing it off may not be the best plan, Ian."

"Sorry."

Warren started another round of chanting moments later, flicking his wand in a figure-eight fashion. Instead of the glowing snowflakes that brought the demon out, this time a black liquid-like substance streamed all over it. It began covering the body from the feet up.

The demon squirmed and groaned, trying to fight against the fluid. Each inch that it covered solidified almost instantly. It was as though Warren was encasing the thing in its final tomb.

"Cast pain at it," Warren yelled.

Rachel and Jasmine turned their shields into wave after wave of lightning-like energy.

Between the black liquid and the burning electricity, I damn near felt sorry for the demon as it fought to get away. Griff's shield held it in place, which I assumed was possible only because the creature was already nearing the end of its life.

With a final push, the pathetic beast screamed at me before being covered in blackness.

It stopped moving and the mages collapsed.

Felicia rushed to Jasmine, Chuck ran over to Griff, and I went to Rachel.

I picked her head off the ground and set it on my lap, brushing the hair out of her face. She was quite a beauty, especially when she wasn't looking at me with incriminating eyes. Her breathing was a steady pant, and sweat glistened lightly on her brow.

The others were in similar situations.

Watching Felicia rub Jasmine's face was kind of hot. Watching Chuck rub Griff's was kind of not.

But, hey, who was I to judge?

Based on the little outburst that just came from that demon, maybe I *did* bone one of its kind at some point. It was pretty tough to tell who or *what* you were boning while in Vegas, after all, especially when you were a bit tipsy at the time.

"Question," Portman said while raising a finger.

"Yes?"

"That demon thing," he said, pointing now at the

encased body lying in our midst. "Is that what's causing these monsters to be all big and powerful?"

"It is," Warren answered for me.

"Uh-huh." Portman was scratching his chin now. "And do they just disappear after a while or something?"

"I don't understand," said Warren.

"He's asking you if it's safe to bring the body back to the morgue," I clarified.

"Not quite," Portman said with a look of concern. "I'm asking because I've already got the other two in the morgue and if they turn all demony like that one just did, I'm going to lose half my goddamn crew!"

CHAPTER 18

$\mathcal{W}$e pulled up to the morgue, which was an abandoned building outside of the city where few dared to tread. The outside was rundown and crumbly, but I'd been here a number of times over my years in the PPD and knew the place looked equally bad inside.

The alarms were already blaring as Portman started bolting for the main door. I yelled out to stop him, but when a dude who turned into a werebear wanted to do something, you tended to let him do it.

"How are your reserves?" I asked Rachel when we got to the door.

"Low," she said.

"Shit."

I looked over at Griff and Jasmine with questioning eyes. They both shook their heads.

That meant we were in for a ride.

If Fido and Captain Vampire had somehow returned to their former, powerful selves, there was no way we could take them down without the combined efforts of my mages. Felicia and Chuck were great fighters, sure, and I could handle myself in a fistfight, too, especially if I called on certain powers that I was loathe to use, but against the likes of these guys, it'd still be tough.

"One of you will have to power the others," I said as a roar sounded from within the building. Portman was in werebear mode. "I don't care who does it, but figure it out and let's get down there."

"I'll handle it," Griff said. "I have the most reserves since I focused on shields during our encounter with the fae." He turned to his partner and said, "Charles, you'll be careful in there, right?"

"Of course," Chuck replied, putting his hand on Griff's shoulder.

"You guys dating or something?" I said with a laugh.

"We are," Griff answered without mirth.

"Oh." I *knew* it! "Cool."

As soon as I shut my big mouth, Griff started to funnel his remaining energy into Rachel and Jasmine. Nothing could be seen except for a minor glow of his hands in theirs. There was no way he'd be able to give them full reserves, but I'd take what I could get.

"Follow us when you're ready," I commanded and then signaled Felicia, Chuck, and Warren to get inside.

We took the steps down to the basement. It seemed logical since the lights were flashing like mad down there and shadows were bolting along the length of the corridor.

I slowed down and pulled out my gun, readying myself

for anything. That's when a massive bear flew past me, heading to my right.

"Portman," I said to the others.

"You sure?" Felicia replied, rolling her eyes at me.

I grimaced and ran after him.

We reached the end of the hallway and found Captain Vampire was up and about again. Right now he was busily battling workers at the morgue. Bodies were littering the floor. Plus, his head had somehow grown back. That was unsettling.

Portman lunged at the vampire, but he was swiped away with relative ease.

"Same drill as last time," I hissed, waving everyone to duck down.

"Shoot him in the groin?" Chuck asked.

"No," I answered after staring at him for a second. "Everyone aim for his head. We just need to stop him long enough for Warren to do one of those black liquid things on him."

We stood up as one and aimed at Captain Vampire's face, unleashing our mags like we were at the range. The glass that separated us from the room shattered and littered the floor. The monster fell backward as his head was blown to bits.

Success!

Sort of.

Standing right behind him was Fido, and he didn't look very happy. And, yes, his head was back on, too.

Good thing Portman had recovered, though, since he cannoned into Fido from the side.

He drove the werewolf into a mass of metal tables that

held cadavers. It wasn't a pretty sight, but it gave us enough time to replace our mags and prepare another volley.

Fido had other plans.

He lifted Portman up and threw him directly at us through the framing of the window we'd just blown out.

On the plus side, since the window was mostly missing, we didn't have to contend with shards of glass stabbing into us; on the other hand, being crushed by the body of a full-grown werebear wasn't exactly a picnic.

Portman scrambled to his feet with a roar as the rest of us lay there wheezing.

Warren had luckily moved far enough out of the way so that only his leg had been hit. This was good, seeing that he wasn't exactly built for physical abuse.

Fido burst through the glass a little farther down and took off back the way we'd originally come in. Portman chased after him with dastardly intentions.

"Warren," I said, my lungs fighting to regain their normal configuration, "get in there and make sure that vampire doesn't come back."

"My leg…"

"Will be the least of your worries if that fucking vampire gets his wits about him."

He gulped. "Right."

"Also, tell any conscious workers to get everyone else out of here."

He nodded and began pulling himself into the room.

Felicia's eyes were glowing red when I finally got her to her feet. She was channeling her inner werewolf. This was good and bad. It was good because it meant she'd have more strength to fight Fido; it was bad because it meant she'd be more likely to go berserk than to think.

Chuck's teeth were elongated, too. This wasn't so terrible, as vampires did just fine unless they got a taste of blood. Seeing that Chuck was a happy drunk, the last thing I needed was for him to take down a pint of Fido's plasma. He'd get all lovey-dovey and end up trying to dance with the enemy instead of fighting to stop them.

"No biting," I warned him with a stern wag of my finger.

"I know, I know," he said, still wincing from the pain of being landed on by a werebear. I then looked at Felicia, and added, "No berserking... or whatever it's called."

"I'm fine," she replied tightly.

I looked down the hall where Portman had just been thrown out of another room. He was *not* having a good day.

"Warren," I called through the frame at the wizard, "follow us when you finish up there."

And with that, the rest of us took off down the hallway after Portman and Fido.

CHAPTER 19

*R*achel and Jasmine joined us as we ran past the stairwell. They both looked a little more energized, which was good considering Fido was bound to be ready for us this time.

"Warren?" asked Rachel.

"He's putting the liquid on our friendly neighborhood vampire," I replied. "Portman is having words with Fido, and the werebear isn't getting very far."

As if on cue, another ferocious roar sounded, followed by the flying body of Portman. But this time something was different. This time there was a massive fireball guiding his path.

"Since when can werewolves do magic?" said Chuck, looking at Felicia.

"It's rare," she answered with a gulp. "Very rare."

"Put that fire out quick," I commanded Jasmine while pointing at Portman.

She cast a spell that quenched the flames on the werebear's chest.

"Ah," came a booming voice from the room that Portman had just been ejected from. "It seems a fellow mage has joined us, my friend."

I took a quick peek around the edge of the window frame and saw a man who was roughly my age. He had long, dirty-blond hair, a neatly trimmed beard, and a body that belonged in a Chippendales calendar. I knew this because he was wearing a pair of jeans topped with a short-sleeved shirt that was unbuttoned.

Plus, I had a very similar body.

"Whoa," said Chuck, who had apparently leaned over to take a look also. "He's pretty hot."

"Seriously?"

"Yeah, seriously. Look at those abs."

I furrowed my brow at him for a moment, but then shrugged at the realization that if the mage standing by Fido had been a chick, I'd be giving her a double-take, too.

At least now I knew who was putting the heads back on these ubernaturals.

"Fair enough," I said finally, "but we still gotta kill him."

He sighed. "Shame."

"While I thank you heartily for the commentary on my abs," the mage called out, "and while I *do* agree with your assessment, I wonder if I might have the pleasure of knowing whom I'm going to be killing?"

I looked at the others and shrugged before stepping out into the open.

"The name's Ian Dex," I said, holding up my PPD badge. "And you are?"

"You may call me Reese, Mr. Dex," he replied with a

genuine smile. "I have to say that your little team has given my... possessions a bit of trouble tonight. I understand your position, of course, but I'm afraid that I'll need to remove you and your fellow officers from the equation now."

"Is that so?" I said, raising my eyebrows.

"Oh, let's not kid ourselves, Mr. Dex. You're clearly no match for me. Yes, you'll likely cause me some mild discomfort, but your genetic splicing is nothing compared to mine."

"You won't just be facing me, Reese," I noted. "And what's that about my genetic splicing, again?"

"I was including your friends in my assessment, Mr. Dex." Portman woke up and shook his head, growling at the same time. Reese glanced over at him. "And your werebear also, of course."

I looked at the mage for a few moments, weighing the situation. He did seem rather confident for a man who was wholly outnumbered. This gave me pause. Was his confidence warranted? He had somehow created these ubernaturals, so clearly he was quite capable with magic. On top of that, they were amalgamations concocted with demons.

My blood froze.

Was that why the demon who had been merged with the fae was pissed off at me? Did my genetic makeup somehow include demons?

"A question before we destroy you?" I said to Reese.

"By all means," he said cordially, "ask away."

"The fae that we destroyed at the Wynn seemed pretty irritated at me because I'm an amalgamite. It didn't really have time to provide details what the deal was, though. Any idea?"

"Demons don't like things they can't inhabit," Reese explained. "They find locked souls to be an affront to the natural order of things."

That was a relief. "So you're saying that I can't be possessed?"

"Is that a problem?" he answered my question with one of his own.

"Quite the contrary," I replied. "Frankly, up until today, I thought all that possession crap was bullshit."

"I assure you it's not," Reese said with a knowing grin.

I nodded at Fido. "Clearly."

"Right." He looked at his watch. "Did you have anything else you wanted to discuss? I do have a schedule to keep."

"Oh, sorry, I was just..." I stopped and frowned at him. "You sure are a confident son of a bitch, aren't you?"

"Supremely," he said as his hands began to radiate blue energy.

"Not again," I cried while diving away from the window.

CHAPTER 20

$\mathcal{M}$y dive didn't do much, except that it may have sufficed in helping me to share the energy that burst from Reese's fingers. Meaning that everyone got hit.

The mages were able to handle it better than the rest of us and they fought back instantly.

Within seconds, the entire place was rocking from energy blasts, fireballs, ice fragments, and things I'd never seen before.

Fido had jumped out and started attacking to support his master.

Mind-over-pain allowed me to empty a magazine through his head, dropping him on the lap of one very angry Felicia.

She exhausted her bullets in what remained of the beast's brain, reloaded, and did it again. When she went for yet another mag, Chuck grabbed her arm and pointed at the room where Reese was laughing his ass off.

"I haven't had this much fun in years," the mad mage yelled while Jasmine and Rachel grunted and groaned.

It was clear they were no match for this guy, and they were already low on power as it was.

Portman was back up, but on fragile footing. He looked even more useless than I felt right now. But to his credit, he roared and lurched in anyway.

I nodded at Felicia and Chuck, pointing at our guns and the window.

None of us were thrilled with the prospect of putting ourselves in line with the mass of magical syrup that was blistering the area, so we crawled along until we found an open spot to fire through.

As one, we stood and unleashed a torrent of breakers at Reese.

It was pointless.

His laughter intensified as he somehow managed to keep it all under control.

Portman was stuck in suspended animation, up on his hind legs with a frustrated scowl apparent on his face. Our bullets were impacting some kind of shield and dropping to the floor like they were nothing.

It was clear that Reese was just toying with my mages. He lowered one hand and fished around in a lunch pail that one of the staff must have brought to work. He pulled out a banana and grimaced at it, throwing it to the side. Next was a tuna fish sandwich, which also seemed to be uninteresting to the bastard. Finally, his eyes lit up and he pulled out a pudding cup. A stream of vile energy poured from his free hand during the entirety of his food scavenging.

To solidify his assholishness, he shouted something that doubled his shield so he could dig into his pudding unabated.

"What a douche," I yelled while climbing through the broken window.

Obviously my bullets weren't going to get through that shield, but maybe I could. I'd considered using one of my special powers at this point, but my hope was it wouldn't be necessary. I hadn't used one in years, and even back then it was for training purposes only.

I spotted a moment of uncertainty on his face as I jumped at the shield.

He threw the pudding cup in my face an instant before I slammed into him. We hit the ground and I started raining down blows as fast as I could.

This gave my team the ability to get in and help me. Portman was also freed from his binds and he was taking a few measured swipes at Reese as well.

The impish mage didn't fight back, though.

He took each punch with only a hint of annoyance as his eyes grew brighter and brighter. He'd obviously cast some type of personal protection spell because it felt like I was punching granite.

On a whim, I whipped out my gun and pressed it against his head, pulling the trigger multiple times.

The breakers were just absorbed and disappeared.

"Move," yelled Rachel, throwing me off and firing spell after spell at the supermodel of a mage.

Jasmine was next to her, sending a stream of energy into Rachel to help keep her powered. Again, though, they were both tiring pretty quickly.

Reese, on the other hand, looked fine.

I'd considered offering Rachel and Jasmine some of that pudding, wondering if that may have helped Reese to maintain his power. Then I realized that was a silly thought.

I looked up and noticed there were a few apparitions floating near the back of the room. I could barely see them, but they were there. They were hazy, shimmering in and out of view. What I *could* make out was the flow of power they were feeding directly into Reese.

"There," I said, grabbing Rachel by the shoulder and pointing.

She tore her glare off Reese and looked up.

"Shit," was all she said as a sound in the room began growing and growing.

It was that tornado type of whooshing that often preceded a massive magical event.

Reese's hands were doing rapid crisscross movements.

"What the hell is he doing?" I yelled, looking back at Rachel while simultaneously jumping at the mage in the hopes that I could stop his hands from continuing.

He was too strong for that.

"It's a..." was all she got out before I was blinded by a massive white flash.

CHAPTER 21

*M*y back smacked the ceiling as the entire room was blown to bits.

I landed with a thud and the world pulsed and jiggled. It was all I could do to keep from passing out.

The feeling reminded me of the time we'd chased down a vampire who was ex-military. Special Forces. We'd had him cornered when he launched a shock grenade into the room. My head rang for days and the disorientation of the concussion lasted weeks.

But there was no time for pain right now. My team was in the shit and I needed to act.

So I did the only thing I could think to do at the time: I stood up and fell over.

My timing was decent, at least, because Reese had thrown a fireball that sailed right past where I would have been had I managed to stay upright.

"I have to hand it to you, Mr. Dex," Reese said as that damn tornado sound began to drone again, "you got much closer to me than I'd anticipated."

While I could understand him, his voice sounded like it was under the influence of a major reverb chamber.

"Glad to have made it interesting for you," I replied, trying to get to my feet.

I did a little better this time, but my balance was so far off that I began running sideways until I crashed into the ground near the door to the room.

Reese unleashed a hearty laugh at this.

"It's truly a shame that I have to kill you all so quickly," he announced. "This has been such fun. Alas, I do have other engagements to attend to."

His eyes were pure white, emanating a glow so strong it looked like a flashlight.

That couldn't possibly be a good thing.

"Get out," I yelled at my crew, who were all suffering the same level of disorientation that I was.

As one, we ran, fell, crawled, and did everything we could to get out of that room.

Reese's laughter grew louder along with the throbbing bounce of magical energy that filled the area.

We had only seconds to get the hell out of there— and not just the room, either. We needed to get out of the building, if not the city!

It looked like we were done for when Warren stepped up, lifted his wand and chanted, firing a bolt of something at the mage who was intent on doing us in.

It struck Reese in the chest and radiated out to whatever the things were that powered him. The whooshing sound dropped to half and Reese's laughter cut off.

"Do it again," I said, but Warren had already fallen to the floor. Wizards aren't exactly what you'd call "robust."

He'd done well, though. He'd covered Fido in black goop and somehow managed to buy us some time to hopefully get the hell out of the building.

The problem was that we were all still more than wobbly, and now we had to carry an unconscious wizard.

I grabbed his arm and started pulling him behind me. Felicia grabbed his other arm, which helped to balance us both out until Portman came along. The werebear was clearly gaining his full faculties already since he merely picked up Warren and ran.

The damn tornado was building and building.

I got to the stairs and directed the others to get out. Whether we bickered or not, they were my crew and their safety was paramount.

Griff was at the top of the stairs waving everyone to hurry up.

Portman roared, taking the stairs in such a way to show he'd fully gathered himself.

"Take," he commanded in a growling voice while handing Warren over.

Griff dragged the scraggly wizard out as Portman padded back down, grabbing up Rachel and Jasmine in his massive arms. He got them out and returned for Felicia and Chuck, who were already near the top of the landing. The werebear dragged them out the rest of the way with a roar.

I grunted with each step as I raced to the last step.

Portman opened the door and reached out for me just as the universe exploded.

CHAPTER 22

I awoke to find I was lying in a white room. There were sounds all around me, but I must have been on some type of medication because everything was fuzzy.

"He's awake, Doctor," said a nice voice that belonged to the cute face of a nurse hovering over me.

The doctor was cuter still. She was the kind you didn't mind giving you an annual physical. I could have gone for a swim in those blue eyes. At least until they flashed slightly, signaling that I was under the care of a mage.

Not that it was necessarily a bad thing for a doctor to be a mage. It's just that I had a reputation in the supernatural community, and I'd been with more than a few doctors, and this one was starting to look familiar.

"Can you hear me, Mr. Dex?" she said.

I went to reply but the dryness in my throat gave way to a cough instead.

"I'll take that as a yes," said the doctor, grabbing a cup

with a straw. I took a few sips. "You had quite a lot of damage, but you seem to be healing fine."

"Yeah, I tend to do that," I croaked out. "My team?"

"They'll all recover," she said, much to my relief.

"Anything serious?"

"The werebear took the most damage," she replied, making it obvious that the nurse was in-the-know about the supernatural community. "His flesh was pretty charred and there are multiple contusions on his face and upper body."

"He saved my crew," I whispered. "Make sure you take good care of him, Doc."

"We always do, Mr. Dex." She flicked at one of the tubes that I assumed was going into my body. "We got word from the Directors that you're all to be fast-tracked. While you heal rather quickly on your own, the rest of your squad is somewhat slower."

"And?"

"And that means that there is a contingent of healers and wizards going from room to room, getting everyone back in tiptop shape." She gave me another sip of water. "You'll be last on their rounds, but you should all be out of here within a couple of hours."

"Good."

"Until then," she commanded, "you need to sleep."

"I can manage that."

"And at some point," she added, leaning in so her face was close to mine, "we'll have to get back together again for another game of doctor-patient."

I gulped.

CHAPTER 23

*T*wo hours later everyone was standing outside of the hospital, looking like nothing had happened to any of us.

I'd honestly not felt this good in years, which made me wonder if getting blown up had been such a bad thing, after all.

"Thanks for getting my team out of that building, Portman," I said to the werebear, who was back to looking like his human self. "Really appreciate it."

"You did the same for my crew."

"Your people got out okay, then?"

"Yeah," he replied. "Most had taken the emergency tunnel as soon as Reese arrived to resuscitate his beasties. The ones caught in the attack got out because of your wizard."

Another checkmark in the "win" column for Warren.

I looked at Portman sideways. "Why do you have an escape tunnel in a morgue?"

"Because things like this used to happen in the old days."

"They did?"

Warren stepped up. "Yes, they did."

"Ah, Warren." I slapped him on the back, thinking that I would put that planning meeting I'd intended to have with him on hold. "Seems the team owes you our thanks. If you hadn't cast whatever it was you did, we'd not be having this conversation."

"Just doing my job, Chief," he said, looking uncomfortable with the attention.

"Well, thanks." I quickly changed the subject back to something that wouldn't fluster him. "So you said that this used to happen in the past. What exactly are you talking about?"

He began rubbing his hands together anxiously as he looked around at all of us.

"It's called 'The Merging,'" he began. "Usually, it's done by a warlock or a witch, but there aren't many of those around these days. Sometimes, though, a mage goes dark and starts using the practice."

"Reese," I stated.

"Right."

"So what does he actually do?" Rachel asked.

"It's the demons," Warren answered. "He summons them for use as batteries, basically."

"We saw that," I noted.

"Yes, but he also merges them with others, typically those who don't see it coming. It's a form of possession."

I rubbed my chin at this. "That would explain why a

little old lady from the finance department would turn into a massive fae."

"Right," Warren said with a nod. "Technically, she was nothing but a vehicle for the demon that possessed her."

"That's no fun." I felt terrible about the fact that we'd essentially turned that poor woman's head into pulp.

"It also means that there are bound to be more of them on the loose," Jasmine put in.

That got my attention. We were all back in working order, and I assumed that the folks the Directors had sent along recharged my mages, but I wasn't exactly in favor of another battle just now. And to think that not 24 hours ago I was complaining about being bored.

"Lydia," I called back to base through the connector, *"have there been any new reports of—"*

"You're okay, baby?" she interrupted in a desperate voice that nearly masked her digitalness.

"Good as new," I replied.

"Thank goodness," came her relieved reply. *"I was so worried about you."*

"Unbelievable," said Rachel while rolling her eyes, and then called out, *"We're okay too, Lydia."*

"That's nice, Agent Cress."

Rachel's eyebrows arched. *"Seriously?"*

"Any new reports of supernaturals doing bad things, Lydia?" I asked before an argument could get started.

"Nothing, honey," she replied, *"but I figured out where that finance seminar was."*

"Oh?"

"You destroyed three supernaturals who were all reported as being out at the conference," she started, *"so I pulled up their*

files with a little help from Turbo and found their vehicle signatures."

"Meaning?"

"They all drive nice cars, sweetie," she said, *"which means they all have GPS. I tracked them down."*

"Where did they go?"

"Behind the Chapel of Flowers."

"Great work, Lydia," I said with a grin. *"You're the best."*

"You can thank me properly later, sugar."

Rachel threw her arms up. "Oh please!"

I stifled a laugh at her jealousy, mostly because I couldn't tell if she was jealous of Lydia or of the fact that Lydia treated me differently. My ego wanted to believe the former, but reality suggested it was the latter.

"Could that Reese guy have even survived that explosion?" Chuck asked. "It was pretty intense."

"Good question," said Felicia. "We barely made it out alive and we'd all gotten pretty far away from the blast point."

"True," said Jasmine, pursing her lips. "But I think Reese is way too powerful to be dumb enough to blow himself up. Besides, he appeared extremely confident in his abilities."

"True, but we did piss him off pretty good," I pointed out. "He wasn't exactly operating under a blanket of calm at the end there."

"That's valid." Jasmine looked thoughtful. "Still, I'd find it hard to believe that he'd be subjected to his own destruction, especially since he knows damn well he's more powerful than us."

We all stood there thinking for a few minutes.

Obviously, we had to assume that Reese survived. To do otherwise would be careless.

"Right," said Portman. "Good luck with catching that bastard, if he's still out there. I gotta bolt."

Portman took off as the rest of us got on the road to check out what was happening behind the Chapel of Flowers.

CHAPTER 24

The Chapel of Flowers was a nice place for couples to tie the knot. It sat about halfway between the old strip and the new, and it had a nice little setup for all sizes of weddings.

But we weren't turning in to the main driveway. We were pulling behind the building next to the convenience store.

There were multiple fancy cars parked there, which looked a bit out of place. Why the vampire, werewolf, and fae didn't drive them away from here, I couldn't say, especially since Fido seemed capable of driving my car without a hitch.

We matched up the licenses and did a little digging into each of the cars.

"I've discovered something," said Griff, holding up a piece of paper that he'd pulled from a white BMW. "It's an invitation and directions. We are definitely in the correct location."

"The chapel or the convenience store?" asked Felicia.

"The parking lot," he answered as he walked around, studying the ground.

"So, let me get this straight," I said while watching him. "Executives from a few major hotels in Las Vegas got invited to a parking lot located between the two strips to talk about finance?"

"Not precisely." Griff held up a finger and then knelt down and traced the symbol that was on the invitation he was holding. The ground shimmered momentarily and a set of stairs appeared. "They met down there."

I glanced around to see if any normals had their eyes on us.

"Don't worry," Griff said, obviously noting my concern. "We're standing in a null zone."

"Ah, good."

Null zones were areas set aside where supernaturals could gather without normals seeing them. There weren't a lot of these places about, and each required strict regulations and proper permitting. It explained why the fancy vehicles were the only thing on this side of the lot. Normals would see an available spot but something would tell them to find somewhere else to park. Null zones were notorious for normals avoiding certain areas due to "gut feelings."

"You think Reese is down there?" I asked.

"Hard to tell," Griff said with a shrug. "There are a plethora of protections around this entire area."

"Anything dangerous?" asked Felicia.

"I would have to defer to our resident wizard."

Warren stepped up and began tracing a symbol in the air. It left behind a little shimmering dust that grew and solidified until it was rather large. Once it stopped growing, it fell and illuminated a set of runes covering the entrance to the underground room.

"Notification runes, mostly," Warren said after a few minutes. "I don't see anything deadly. At least not up here."

"Can you nullify them?" I asked, not really wanting to have another run-in with Reese until we knew more about what he was up to.

"Give me a few minutes."

As Warren worked on dispelling the runes, I spoke with the rest of the crew regarding our next encounter with the lovable demon-wielding mage.

"The only way we're going to have a shot at taking him down is if we knock out his power supply," Rachel stated as fact. "Jasmine and I combined our energies and it was like a gnat fighting a dinosaur. He's just far too powerful for us." She then winked at Jasmine. "Plus, he was pretty hot."

Jasmine nodded. "I'll say."

"Hard to argue that," agreed Felicia. "I prefer dark-haired guys, but there's no arguing Reese is one hell of a good-looking man."

"Word," said Chuck, and then glanced up at Griff. "Sorry."

Griff grimaced in response and then sighed.

While the rest of us had been impacted with strong libidos due to the genetic enhancements we received upon joining the PPD, Griff's properness kept him from engaging in our often juvenile rhetoric. Everyone was warned that not only would their personal skills and aggression increase after they were genetically modified, but so too would their sexual desire. It wasn't like any of us joined the PPD unawares. There was even a document we had to sign that absolved the PPD from lawsuits and such. This was because we'd be working together and things were bound to… happen. Still, I seemed to get the best of it, though the rest of them probably considered that I got the worst.

"Right," I said, breaking the tension. "Now that we've agreed on how studly that bastard of a mage is…."

"You think he looked studly, too, eh?" teased Rachel.

"Har har," I replied, using one of the very few chances I got to roll my eyes at her. "Point is that he's going to turn up at some point. Our bullets are pretty useless against him, though maybe my Desert Eagle will up the threat a little."

"You're getting an Eagle?" said Felicia.

"Already been requisitioned. Rachel's getting one, too."

"What about the rest of us?" asked Chuck. "I'm not going to be running around with a pea shooter if you're carrying a portable cannon."

"Ask Lydia to get you one," I said. "Anyone else want one?" Their hands all went up, except for Griff's. "Okay, okay. Put in the request and I'll approve it. We're going to need to get Turbo to build us up some ammo for them though."

"Guns are so uncivilized," chided Griff as Warren waved his hand at me.

"You want a Desert Eagle, Warren?" I said, shaking my head at him. "I gotta say that I'm surprised at that. You'll need to take shooting lessons, though, because it's not like pointing a wand."

Warren furrowed his brow and scratched his beard for a moment. "I don't know what a Desert Eagle is, Chief, and I certainly have no interest in taking shooting lessons."

"Oh… I thought you wanted a gun like everyone else."

"No, thanks," he said, sitting up in shock. "Those things are uncivilized."

I looked up at Griff. These two must have been reading from the same book.

"Says the guy who puts black goo all over demons," noted Felicia.

"I had no choice. If I had—"

"Let it go, Warren," I interrupted. "She's just trolling you."

"Ah."

"What did you want to tell me?"

"I've cleared out all the runes," he replied, "but there's nothing else down there."

"Nothing?"

"It's completely empty."

"Damn."

CHAPTER 25

We'd all climbed down to the room below to have a look around. Sure enough, the place was devoid of anything. No chairs, no filing cabinets, no carpet, no pipes. Nothing. It was just a 20x20 gathering place.

"Any residual power signatures?" Rachel asked as she studied one of the walls.

Warren gave her an appraising look and then started tracing another symbol in the air. While I loved wizards, especially ones with the ability to save me and my crew from an exploding building, they were rather slow. I know this all stemmed from the fact that their spells were intricate, required a lot of study and patience, and didn't allow for mistakes. Mistakes could be very bad indeed. But I wasn't exactly known for my patience.

"There were many lifeforms here within the last twenty-four hours," he said finally, pointing at a set of spheres that hovered where I'd assumed people had been standing. "Based on the colors and luminosity of each, I'd say we have a vampire, a fae, two werewolves, and a succubus."

I looked up, seeing all eyes on me, except for Warren's. He was still moving around the scene.

"What?" I said. They collectively shook their heads. "What?" I said again, this time with more fervor.

"There are also a few very powerful signatures here," Warren continued as he knelt down near an orb that was glowing a red so dark that it nearly looked black. "This is a demon." He jabbed his finger in the air at the rest of the red spheres. "There are nine in total."

"Three of which have already been eradicated by your black goop stuff, right?" I asked hopefully as I tried to redirect everyone's thoughts back to the issue at hand.

"That would be my guess," he said. "Which means we've still got six unaccounted for, and that's only assuming they were all down here to begin with."

The orbs were slowly starting to fade as Warren moved to the largest of them all. It was bright white with traces of black and green spinning tightly in its center. There was a mix of beauty and horror to it.

"How many demons did you see acting as batteries?" Jasmine asked Rachel and me. "Please say six."

"I only saw three," I replied.

"Four," Rachel said once I'd finished. "The fourth one was behind the outer wall."

"It was?"

"You couldn't have seen it, Ian," she noted. "Your eyes are great in the dark, but they're not much for spotting energy signatures through concrete."

"Right."

"This last one must belong to the mage," Warren said in a voice laced with awe. By now the rest of the orbs had all but disappeared. "I've never seen a signature this powerful before. It's… scary."

"So was the dude himself," Chuck quickly pointed out. "And if he's still on the loose, we'd better hunt him down quick or we'll be in a world of hurt pretty damn soon."

"Agreed." I started climbing out of the meeting place. I didn't much enjoy being trapped in enclosed spaces. "Let's get back to base, pick up our new weapons, and head out in the field before night closes in. My gut says that this Reese guy works primarily at night."

"Don't most of our kind?" Rachel said.

"Yep. Thank goodness."

"Just a moment," Griff called out as I approached the driver's side of the Aston Martin. "We've picked through the vehicles here, and we know about the three people we've already dispatched, but there was another werewolf and a succubus on the list that Warren gave out."

"So?" said Chuck.

"So we have two more cars here."

"Ah," I said, snapping my fingers. "Run the plates and we can figure out who the other two are. Maybe we can make a move on them before they start behaving badly."

"Indeed," Griff agreed.

I got back on the connector with Lydia and asked her to get in to central and figure out who the owners of the vehicles were.

"*Jeffrey Case and Brittany Miller,*" she replied almost instantly. "*Sorry, puddin', but I already picked up the signals on the GPS units next to the cars I'd tracked and then did a loop back on them."*

"Excellent," I said. *"Any trace of where they went?"*

"I've put in calls to their superiors, babycakes. They've not been seen nor heard from since leaving for the seminar."

"You're really amazing, Lydia, you know that?"

"You just make it easy on me, lover."

Rachel said, "I think I'm going to be sick," and then got in the car.

I smiled at that and glanced around at the others.

"We can't do anything until Reese and his baddies show up again, so let's head back to base and pick up our new weapons."

CHAPTER 26

Everyone had received their Desert Eagles. They were beautiful. Deadly, but beautiful.

It was a little heavy without a payload, but staring at this gem was enough to know I'd get used to it.

Turbo, who was like the non-douche version of EQK, had brought us in and was showing us the new ammo. It looked like a standard mag setup with a seven-round maximum. He'd built out the breakers to conform to the 50-caliber specs, and they were quite large.

"Each one is imbued with both silvers and woods," he said with an excitement level that only pixies could muster. It probably had to do with their tiny statures and their never-ending supply of energy. "I also mixed negation strands in there."

"Seriously?" I said with wide eyes—the kind of eyes you got as a kid when your parents had a bike sitting by the tree on Christmas. "You mean I don't have to pick and choose anymore?"

"Nope!" He pushed up his Coke-bottle glasses and

smiled wide. "Frankly, though, you probably don't need the breakers at all. This gun is like a mini cannon!"

I stared lovingly at the beast. The gun, not the pixie. Turbo wasn't my type. The gun was. It had a six-inch barrel, black finish, combat sights, and it fit my hand like Serena's hips. I glanced up at the crew reflexively at that little fantasy, thinking it would be best to never mention that fact aloud.

"I've also added in a field stabilization system and a full dampener."

"What's that for?" asked Chuck, who was playing a game of quick draw with his Eagle.

"Silences it and reduces the kick of the weapon," answered Turbo as his wings flapped even faster. "Firing those guns without one of those will wake up half the city!"

I thought I'd been in love with the thing before, but having a gentle recoil and a silencer built in only added to my infatuation.

"Turbo," I said, "you're a genius."

"Aw, shucks," he replied, waving a dismissive hand at me. "I know."

We went to put on headgear so we could start firing, but Turbo shook his head at us. It was hard to believe that we wouldn't need ear protection, but I'd never known the little guy to steer us wrong. Even if the crack of gunpowder exploding in the chamber *was* loud, my ears would heal soon enough. It was everyone else's ears I was seeking to protect.

I leveled the gun, noting quite a weight difference between it and my standard weapon. There would definitely be an adjustment period. But I got the feeling that I only needed to fire in the general vicinity of whatever I wanted to hit. The wind alone would probably kill an ogre.

I lined up my shot, aiming at the gel-based target that sat twenty-five feet out.

The trigger action was so smooth that it reminded me of getting in a new car and stepping on the brakes. The first time you did it, the car would lurch so much that you nearly kissed the steering wheel. There was only the faintest popping sound and almost no kick at all. But the target damn near exploded on impact.

My jaw dropped open at the sight of all the silver and wood shards that filled the gel from edge to edge. With my old weapon, there was a decent spread, but this thing damn near sent bits flying straight out of the target. I focused my vision tighter and spotted the worming black shards as they continued meandering through the gel. Nasty.

"Damn," I heard Rachel say. "I don't know that I can approve of using this thing."

"What do you mean?" I asked, stepping back from the partition slightly. "I think it's great."

Her face was almost completely white. "For monsters like we've been fighting recently, sure. But we can't fire these at just anyone."

"Why would you go around firing at people?" I asked.

"I mean criminals, you walnut."

"Oh, right."

She had a point. Against beasties like Fido, it was almost a requirement to have a gun like the Eagle on your side. But for your average, everyday villain, it was overkill. Literally.

"So we'll carry both."

"I think I'll stick with magic," she said, putting down the weapon. "I thought I'd feel differently about it, but it's just too much for me."

"Okay. You *are* still planning to carry a knife around in your boot, though, right?"

"Of course," she said, grimacing. "I'm not an idiot."

Jasmine followed suit. Griff nodded knowingly at them as they all exited the room.

This wasn't completely unexpected, being that they were mages. Again, they still had their own weapons of choice, but a Desert Eagle was apparently beyond the scope of what they'd deemed reasonable.

"Hey, Turbo," I said while rubbing my chin, "could you make mini versions of these bullets for the smaller guns? I hate having to worry about moving from silvers to woods all the time."

"Great idea!"

Felicia, Chuck, and I spent the next half hour firing the things into gels and models of werewolves, vampires, zombies, and all sorts of beasties.

I could have stayed there for many hours, but as fate would have it, that wasn't an option.

It was time to update the Directors.

CHAPTER 27

*I*t was the same routine as before. The same as always. I sat in a chair while the Directors asked questions. Sometimes they fed me information; most of the time they didn't.

"You're certain that this is happening due to a merging?" asked O.

"That's what my lead wizard suspects, sir," I answered. "Honestly, I haven't any idea since magic isn't one of my strong suits."

"It's not as weak in you as you may believe."

"This isn't time for a lesson, O," Silver pointed out while leaning forward. "How were the demons destroyed?"

"Warren used some type of black liquid on them, sir. Said it had something to do with a void."

"Permanent death," Silver said, leaning back again.

"What does that mean?" asked Zack.

Silver whispered, "Exactly what it sounds like."

The panel grew quiet for a few moments. That

happened now and then. I guessed they used a cone of silence or something so I couldn't hear what they were talking about. This time, though, I could make out the rhythmic tapping of Zack's hand on the table.

"Sorry," I said, unable to contain myself, "but you're saying that whole 'permanent death' thing like it's a negative, sir. We *are* talking about demons here, right?"

"Just because something is a demon does not make it inherently bad," O answered.

I squinted. "But they're... demons."

"And on the panel before you is a vampire, a werewolf, a mage, and a pixie. Are we not bantered about in standard texts as being evil as well?" O then coughed. "Okay, maybe not the pixie as much, but they never had to contend with one like ours."

He had a point. Every piece of mythology pointed out the negatives regarding the supernaturals. To be fair, usually when a normal had the unfortunate experience of meeting a supernatural, things didn't go so swimmingly. Still, criminals were the minority. Most supernaturals were just trying to get by, make a living, and raise their own little vampires and werewolves and such.

"Fair enough," I said.

"You can both stick it up your own asses," EQK retaliated. "Or each other's asses, for all I care."

"Um," I replied, squinting in his general direction. "Ew."

"How many are left?" asked Zack.

"Asses?"

"No, EQK," Zack said with a hint of menace, "I'm asking Mr. Dex how many demons remain."

"Six, sir," I replied before the pixie could blurt something else out. "We believe that two of them are already merged and the other four are acting as a battery for Reese."

"A battery?" said Silver.

"Rachel said that he's drawing power from them somehow." I wiped my forehead with my sleeve. "The guy is already way more powerful than my crew, sir, but at the rate he throws out energy, he should be exhausted in less than a minute. The demons funnel strength his way. It's like he's got no end to his supply."

Another round of silence followed. I was starting to get the feeling that I was the one on trial here. Did Paula from The Spin get in touch with these guys and tell them to open a can of whoop-ass on me or something? Besides, why weren't they doing something about this themselves? I mean, sure it was my jurisdiction and I was the chief here, but they knew damn well that I only had a handful of officers to deal with this sort of thing. We were meant for managing the occasional werewolf tearing up the town or guys like that vampire who, through a moment of weakness, bit into a normal's neck. Dealing with someone like Reese and his ubernaturals was on the edge of our capabilities, regardless of our collective genetic make-up.

"How are you planning to stop him?" Zack asked.

"Honestly," I said as my ire continued to climb, "I have no idea."

"This is unsettling," said O.

"Ya think?"

The panel silenced, letting me know I'd overstepped

my bounds. This happened now and then. But this time there was more to it than me just being me.

"Look, I'm sorry," I said, sitting up and placing my elbows on the table, "but this Reese character is tough to tackle. He kicked our butts like we were nothing. One of him using demon batteries against my entire team and we didn't even have a chance."

They were still silent. Pompous fuckers.

"I honestly expected a bit more out of you than 'This is unsettling.'"

"Such as?"

"I don't know," I said, letting it all out. "How about stepping out from behind that pedestal of yours and giving us some goddamn help? You guys are supposed to be big and powerful. I know that we have enhanced capabilities as part of our deal with being members of the PPD, but you guys are the cream of the crop." I crossed my arms in the hopes of solidifying my point. "Honestly, we could use some muscle here."

I guess one of the major aspects of maturity was taking your time to think through your words before blurting them. The panel always sat in silence after I went on a rant, signaling that their level of maturity far exceeded mine.

"We are incapable of coming to your aid, Mr. Dex," O said softly.

"Why?"

"Because we're nowhere near you," Zack answered. "You're not the only precinct where we sit on the board."

"Oh." I'd honestly never considered that. "Where are you?"

"All over the place," said Silver. "I'm in St. Louis, O is in New York, Zack is in Boston, and EQK is in Seattle."

"I see." I licked my lips, feeling a bit foolish at the moment. "Well, my apologies then."

"No," said O after a moment, "your frustration is understandable."

I nodded. "Thanks. Okay, so aside from the standard 'do your best' advice, would you have *any* concrete suggestions?"

"Shoot him in the cock?" blurted EQK, demonstrating yet again that I wasn't the only one in the room who suffered from immaturity. "It worked last time!"

CHAPTER 28

*N*ight had finally rolled in, signaling the action was going to start soon, assuming Reese had survived his own tantrum at the morgue.

I dispatched Chuck and Griff to Old Town to search for Jeffrey Case, who happened to work at the Downtown Grand. Felicia and Jasmine headed to The Mirage where Brittany Miller worked. Financier by day, succubus by night. My kind of woman.

Rachel and I canvased the main strip, looking for anything unusual.

While we had the basic stats on the two remaining seminar attendees, we still had no idea where and when Reese was going to turn up. We had a bit of an edge because he likely assumed we were dead. Unless, of course, he had an informant somewhere.

Serena and Warren had gone with Felicia because the wizard preferred the Camaro over my Aston Martin. I had the Rapide S, so there *was* a back seat, but he claimed there was more room for him to prepare in the muscle car. How he could prepare for anything while sliding around in the back of that thing was beyond me. My guess was that he had a thing for Jasmine. Couldn't blame him since I did too. Of course, I also had a thing for Rachel, Felicia, and Serena.

"What did the Directors say?" Rachel asked off the connector.

"Same thing they always say. 'Do your best' or some shit like that. Now and then they'll give me a solid piece of help, but mostly it's just me providing status reports and feeling like I'm being judged."

She nodded as I turned left on West Tropicana and past the Hooters Casino Hotel. To my credit, I didn't look at the girls standing outside.

"I was talking with Warren while you were in the meeting," she said. "He's got an idea that may just work, but it's not going to be easy for him to manage."

"Is that why Serena's with him?"

"She's good at keeping his emotions in check."

"She's good at a lot of things."

Rachel shook her head. "You need help."

"Probably," I replied, feeling like a heel. "Listen..."

"No, thanks."

"Seriously, just hear me out."

She uncrossed her arms and groaned. Then she motioned me to go on.

"You guys all got genetically enhanced when you joined the PPD, so you got the horny gene just like I did. But there's something different about me."

"That's true."

"Play nice," I warned. "I'm trying to open up here."

"Go on."

"Well, it's just that you hit level eleven mage overnight, just like Jasmine and Griff. Warren is slow as crap, but his abilities as a wizard are pretty ridiculous. Felicia can control her werewolf side better than most any werewolf out there, even those holding the highest seats. Same with Chuck and Serena with their vampireness." I swallowed. "But I'm different than you all. I never got direct enhancements."

"Could have fooled me," she said.

"I'm not talking about *that*," I said irritably. Wasn't I supposed to be the juvenile one here? "I'm talking about the fact that I'm an amalgamite. I'm different. Vastly so. My genetic splicing was across the board. Yours was directed at a single facet of your abilities. Where you got one magnitude of rowdy plaything added to your genome, I got ten."

"Okay, okay," she said. "Fair enough."

"Wait, I'm not finished." This took some effort. "When you have a mage issue, you have someone to talk to. For example, when Felicia is having her monthly thing—"

"What?"

We stopped at a light and I gave her a look. "I'm talking about the full moon event, Rachel. Werewolf stuff."

"Oh, right. Sorry, I was…" She coughed lightly. "You were saying?"

"My point is that you all have someone to turn to whenever you're confused, lost, or just need an ear to bend who understands what you're going through." The light changed and I cut left on Swenson in order to circle back toward the strip. "I've got nobody."

Neither of us said anything as I continued driving along. I drove past the sports fields of the University of Las Vegas until finally taking a left on East Flamingo.

"Honestly," she said, "I've never thought about it that way."

"We've been partners for seven years, Rachel."

"And you've been a player that entire time."

"True," I said. "Again, though, I'm kind of built that way."

"Yeah, I know." It wasn't said with malice, which was something new. "I guess in some respects we're all a bit jealous of you."

"Of me?" I couldn't help but laugh at that.

"I'm being straight up here, Ian. You're kind of like a jack of all trades."

"Master of none."

"I don't know," she said. "You *are* pretty damn good at one thing."

"Hard to argue that," I said, giving her a quick wink.

"I'm talking about leading this team."

"Oh, right."

We passed the Silver Sevens and began creeping up on the Tuscany Suites.

It was a nice night on the strip. The sky was clear and the air was just warm enough to feel good without pushing into sweat territory. I was tempted to put down the windows as Fido had done the night before, but I knew that Rachel would just get irritated at me. She was an air conditioner kind of woman.

"You have a knack for it," she continued. "And while you also have a tendency of saying the wrong thing most of the time, everybody knows that you'll do what needs to be done in order to protect us."

"Well, of course. You're my team."

"I know that's how you feel, Ian," she said, nodding. "Believe it or not, though, there are many people out there who talk the talk without a problem, but when it comes time to walk the walk, they only look out for number one."

She was right, of course. There were many kinds of leaders in the world. Some always had your back. They took the heat when you screwed up, and then they gave you a little taste of that heat so you could learn and improve. Some let the heat flow straight through. There were others who did all they could to protect their own hides even if it meant sacrificing everyone under them in the process.

"I appreciate it," I said, which was admittedly difficult. "Just know that I'm not likely to change. I like the ladies and I like living somewhat lavishly. It's who I am."

"And you remember that we're here to point out that you're an asshole whenever you do that."

I smiled genuinely. "Fair enough."

With Bally's on the left and the Flamingo on the right, I knew we'd gotten back to South Las Vegas Boulevard.

We went south again and cruised down a ways until we passed the CityCenter and started coming up to The Park and New York-New York.

"It's getting pretty late," I said to the entire team through the connector as I got my head back in the game.

"I've a feeling the shit's going to hit the fan pretty soon. If you spot anything, don't engage alone. It'll be far easier for us to attack those damn things as a team."

"I don't think they're going to find anything," Rachel said while leaning a bit forward in the passenger seat.

"Why not?"

She pointed to the top of the Excalibur.

There was a massive light show of magic going on.

We had found Reese.

CHAPTER 29

*R*eese hadn't gotten into full power mode yet, thankfully.

Felicia and Jasmine had turned up with Warren and Serena, but we were still waiting on Griff and Chuck. They were halfway here and I was itching to go up and get the show rolling. We needed everyone, though, so I held myself in check.

"What's the plan, Warren?" I asked, trying to pass the time.

"I need to study this right now, Chief," he answered.

Serena stepped over and took me by the arm. She walked me a few feet away.

"He's a little sensitive," she said in her sultry voice. "His plan is to build a set of runes that will cut the ability for the demons to feed power to Reese."

"That sounds good."

"Yes, but it will take some time, and he knows how that irritates you."

"Only because I'm usually in the process of being killed when he's doing it."

"I know, darling," she said, running a finger through my hair. "Like I said, he's sensitive."

So was I at the moment.

Serena loved playing the game as much as I did. In fact, I often wondered if there was more to her alterations than met the eye. Regardless, now was not the time for love. Later, yes. Definitely later. Now, though, I had to focus, which I guess was exactly what Warren was trying to do.

With much effort, I smiled at Serena and said, "You should probably keep helping him. I'll stay out of his hair and will *try* to be as patient as possible."

Jasmine and Rachel were discussing their tactics as well. It seemed to me that the majority of what they did was throw fireballs, ice balls, ice storms, and put up shields, but they always discussed their plans anyway.

I shrugged and moved over to Felicia. At least she was somewhat like me, meaning that she was more physical when it came to fighting. She had that werewolf blood, too. It made her act in primal fashion.

"Ready for this?" I said.

The reddish color of her eyes answered before she did. "Yep."

"Between you and me, Felicia, I'm not sure if we're going to get out of this one."

"I didn't think we'd get out of the last one either."

"We shouldn't have."

"I know." She leaned in, releasing a low growl. "We have time for a quickie."

"Are you serious?" I said, giving her a look that said, 'Didn't you want to punch me in the neck not long ago because you thought I was a freak?'

She provided a look of her own and then said, "Hey, we're about to die, right?"

"Probably," I said, feeling suddenly nervous. "But for reasons that I can't quite explain, I'm not in the mood."

"That's new."

"I know, right?"

She sighed. "Suit yourself. I'm going to go play some slots."

Just as she dropped in a coin and pulled the handle, Griff and Chuck came through the main entrance. Chuck was running as Griff followed him briskly.

"Sorry," Chuck said, "we got here as fast as we could."

"We wished to verify that the other werewolf hadn't stayed over in the old strip to create a diversion," Griff added.

I looked them both over. "And you're sure he didn't?"

"No," admitted Griff, "but after a solid look around we felt it more wise for us to be here to assist with Reese. He is quantifiably more powerful than a single ubernatural."

"Valid point."

I gathered everyone up and started walking toward the main security station. We flashed our badges and were immediately let through to the back areas. A hidden elevator shaft opened up with buttons that could take us to the top floor. From there it would be a quick climb onto the roof via an access stairwell.

How Reese and his goons had gotten up there, I had

no idea. I just knew that they were on top of the tall building that sat parallel to Tropicana Avenue.

We stepped out onto the roof and snuck around past the massive machinery until we could see our wizard pal, a werewolf, a succubus, and four apparitions that were obviously the demons.

"I hope you're all ready," I said.

Their determined looks were the only response I needed.

CHAPTER 30

*M*y first thought was to take out my Eagle and just place a nice 50-caliber round through Reese's skull, but I was positive he'd have some type of shielding up already. If we tipped our hand too soon, we'd be flat on our asses.

So we moved slowly, keeping behind the pieces of equipment that littered the roof.

Reese was facing away from us while his minions were looking at him. There were lights and flashes of energy swarming around all of them like some type of wicked vortex. I had no idea what they were doing, but I couldn't imagine that it would be good for the people of Las Vegas.

"Keep your heads down," I said in hushed tones over the connector. *"Warren, take your damn hat off. You look like an air conditioner shark."*

Some people just weren't built for this kind of work.

"Oops," he said. *"Sorry."*

The goal was to get Warren and Serena as close as

possible so they could put down the demon-crushing runes, but I had this feeling it wasn't going to be easy.

"*This would be much simpler if I could just set these runes up underneath him,*" Warren said.

I glanced at Rachel and sighed. She merely shrugged in return. I forced myself to remember that Warren had recently saved our butts.

"*Everyone stop,*" I commanded. They did. "*Warren, are you saying that these runes would work from underneath him?*"

"*They should.*"

"*Honestly, man, you really need to let us know about these things ahead of time.*"

"*Sorry,*" he said again.

We slunk back to the access door and climbed inside. I wanted to smack Warren around a bit, but I held myself in check. Right now we had a job to do.

"Where exactly do you need to be?" I asked.

"Under them."

"So go down a level and you've got that."

"Sorry," he said, fidgeting. "I mean I have to be *directly* under them."

"They're pretty spread out," Rachel noted. "It's not like there are a bunch of rooms all connected without walls."

"Well," Warren said as if Rachel were stupid, "it doesn't have to be *directly* under them."

"You literally just said it did," Rachel countered.

"You're right, I did say that." He was starting to get flustered. "It has to be close enough."

"What's the radius?" I asked, fighting my annoyance. "Just a ballpark figure is fine."

"A couple hundred feet," he said with a shrug and a look of uncertainty.

"So you're not sure."

It was a statement, not a question.

The fact was that wizardry wasn't an exact science. This is why it took so long to enact spells, and also why people like Warren were somewhat odd. They had to be in order to navigate the puzzles that made up a wizard's brand of magic. Powerful, certainly, but also imprecise if not carefully managed. How a guy who couldn't even comprehend that a tall, pointy hat was not conducive to being stealthy could possibly manage the intricacies of these things was a mystery to me. Funny that most wizards were just like him, though.

"*Lydia,*" I called back to base, "*can you check if there are any available rooms on the top floor of the Excalibur, Tropicana Avenue side?*"

"*Certainly, puddin',*" she replied. "*Just a moment.*"

With our luck, there'd be no availability. That meant we'd either have to sneak in or take over someone's room. I hated having to do it, but some things just couldn't be helped.

"*All booked up, honey,*" she said, confirming my expectations.

"*Of course they are.*" I pinched the bridge of my nose. "*Any chance there are some nice suites available somewhere?*"

There was another pause. "*There is a two-bedroom luxury suite available.*"

"*Perfect,*" I said with a sense of relief. "*Notify the front desk that they are upgrading the people at the far end of the top floor. Give them the PPD numbers and tell them to be quick about it!"*

"*You got it, baby,*" she said with a coo. "*I love it when you act forceful.*"

Rachel face-palmed.

CHAPTER 31

*T*he young couple that was escorted away from the room looked like they'd just won the lottery. I had no idea what the hotel told them, but the manager gave me a nod as he went by, letting me know that the couple would be none the wiser.

A swarm of hotel staff hit the room for two minutes before we were allowed in.

As they left, one of the bellhops handed me a keycard and rubbed his white-gloved fingers together.

"Seriously?" I said to his expectant face.

Rachel laughed as I forked over a twenty-dollar bill to the guy.

"Honestly, you *do* realize that we're PPD, right?"

"I have no idea what that is, sir," he said, "but I hope you all have a wonderful stay at the Excalibur."

When I walked into the room, Warren was standing on a credenza that sat by the television. He was tracing little lines on the ceiling. Serena was standing nearby with the looks of someone ready to catch him, should he fall.

Being that it was Warren, there was a fair amount of validity in that fear.

"We should probably get him a ladder," suggested Chuck. "Want me to call down to the front desk and ask for one?"

"Good idea," I said, tucking my wallet away.

A few minutes later a worker brought up a step ladder, which resulted in me pulling my wallet back out. I had little doubt that I would not be able to expense these tips. Not that I needed to, but it was the principle of the thing.

"So?" I said, feeling a bit perturbed. "What's the deal?"

Warren held up a finger as he finished whatever it was he was tracing.

The ceiling shimmered briefly before becoming nearly transparent. We were suddenly looking up at the night sky. It wasn't like a window or anything, but it was clear enough to be rather amazing.

"Holy shit," I said, moving to stand under the succubus.

Rachel slapped me on the shoulder. "Freak."

"What?"

"This *is* a one-way window, right?" asked Jasmine.

"Yes, definitely," replied Warren. Then he quickly glanced over his iPad with a look of horror. Finally, he relaxed and repeated, "Yes."

We all released a concerned breath.

Wizards.

I tore myself away from the vision of the succubus. This wasn't easy considering she was like a succubus on steroids. Where all the other merged beasties had been rather unfortunate looking, except maybe the vampire, this chick was smoking hot. Her eyes glowed like diamonds, her hair flowed like a river, her skin glistened like the finest dew on a morning leaf, and her glutes were so tight that I imagined she could crush a walnut between them. My thoughts grew poetic in the face of perfection.

Shaking my head, I said, "Right, so what's the plan?"

"I need to think," Warren said.

"And you can do that as soon as you tell us the plan, Warren."

"Hmmm?" he said with a confused look. "Oh, right. Well, I'm going to put together a complete rune set that will stop those demons from funneling power to Reese."

"Yes, I got that," I said, clearly needing him to be more specific. "What I'm asking is how you're going to do that and how long will it take?"

"Right, okay," he said, pointing around. "I have to fill the ceiling with runes. The entire thing will be covered. It'll take me about an hour, if I have complete silence."

"So…"

"So," Rachel said, motioning everyone toward the door, "we have to leave."

"Except for Serena," Warren stated. "I need her to help me."

I nodded, sad to have been leaving the room. Then I gave one more look up at the succubus of my dreams. Granted, she would not be so attractive in about an hour, since she'd be trying to rip my soul to shreds, and not in a good way. But for now she was quite a vision.

"Are you done?" Rachel asked as she, Felicia, Griff, and Jasmine all shook their heads at me.

I sighed and walked out of the room.

CHAPTER 32

We'd decided that the best course of action was to get back up to the roof and keep tabs on Reese's progress. I preferred not to engage until Warren had the demons under control, but that meant we had to be careful about being spotted.

There was no way to know precisely what Reese was up to. Nobody on my team expected it to be pleasant, though. Regardless of what the Directors had to say about demons, in their current manifestation they had nefarious intentions. I couldn't say if that was due to Reese's manipulations or not, but in the grand scheme of things that didn't matter right now.

"Let's take it slow," I commanded through the connector. *"Anything we can do ahead of time to make this easier, do it. Just don't tip our hand in the process."*

We crept along the roof. It was a solid distance to the other side since we had to move along the length of the building to the corner first.

I glanced at the powerful mage every few feet to make sure we'd not been spotted.

In some respects the layout up here was perfect for stealth. We had decent cover behind the massive ventilation units and their incessant humming covered any missteps. I didn't expect anyone to trip up in this group, especially with Warren not actively moving along with us. Still, it was nice to have some measure of protection from prying eyes.

"This feels too easy," Rachel whispered to me. "I don't like it."

I paused.

"What do you mean?"

"He's a pretty powerful guy, right?"

"Obviously."

"So why would he just have his back to the vast majority of the roof like this?"

She had a point, but there was something about this Reese guy that told me there was a logical explanation.

Ego.

"Think like him for a second," I said as we resumed our move to the center building that sat at the elbow of the roof. "He blew the crap out of the morgue earlier and probably assumes we were all killed in the process. Plus, he's got demons and ubernaturals to cover his ass and give him an unlimited supply of power."

"Possibly," she said, looking unconvinced.

"Even if he thinks we survived it, he knocked us out with relative ease." I shook my head, remembering the thrashing we'd gotten. "He kicked the shit out of us, Rachel. That's not easy to do."

"True, but he's also got to think that there are more of us than just a small unit."

"Unless he's done his homework," I argued. "It wouldn't take much to find out that the Las Vegas branch of the PPD has a limited set of officers." I sneered. "Damn cutbacks. And he *did* know my name, remember?"

"Again, true," she agreed. "Still, something tells me we're walking into trouble here."

"Well, duh," I replied with a laugh. "I don't care if we have twenty officers, this isn't going to be joyous by any stretch of the imagination. Not only do we have to deal with Admiral Psycho and The Four Demon Batteries—"

"A band name?" she interrupted with a roll of her eyes. "You're giving them a band name?"

"Seemed fitting." I shrugged. "Anyway, he's also got a werewolf and a succubus that we have to contend with."

Everyone arrived at the center building and sat with their backs along the wall. Chuck was peeking around the outer edge and Felicia kept watch from the other side.

Reese could be heard yelling what I assumed were commands in demon-tongue. It was a guttural-sounding language with an occasional high-pitched squeak. In some respects, it sounded rather ridiculous.

"Anyone know what he's saying?" I asked in a quiet voice, feeling confident that the big machines were enough white noise to make it so Reese couldn't hear me.

"He is planning to take over the world," Griff answered. "I can only understand snippets of it. Jasmine or Rachel may know more."

They both shook their heads.

"Right." Griff closed his eyes as we all sat silently. "He

will take over our city first. Then he plans to fully tap our magic lines. He'll merge all of the vampires, werewolves, and the rest." Griff's eyes snapped open. "Essentially, the man is building a demon army."

"Sounds like it," I said, fighting not to call Griff "Captain Obvious" in the process. "Obviously we can't let that happen."

"Ya sure, Captain Obvious?" said Rachel.

I gave her my best duck-face.

"What's our move, Chief?" said Chuck.

"Same as before," I said while continuing to hold my frown at a grinning Rachel. "We wait."

CHAPTER 33

Unfortunately, from Griff's play-by-play of Reese's rallying cry to the demons, it was about time for them to start causing trouble.

"...and it looks like they're just waiting for the moon to be directly overhead."

I looked up. It seemed close enough to me, but I was guessing that Reese or the demons or a combination of both had some power gauge to make a better determination.

"Anyone have any idea how much time it'll be before that happens?"

"I'd guess about thirty minutes," said Jasmine.

"Sounds about right," agreed Rachel.

I thought to ask how they could tell, but figured I'd get some explanation about the way the power lines pulsed against a coming herd of unicorns or something else that would be senseless to me. Instead, I decided it was time to see how far along Warren and Serena were with their project.

"*Warren,*" I called through the connector, "*how are things going with the runes?*"

"*They were going pretty well until you just startled me, Chief,*" he said. "*I'll have to redo that one.*"

"*Sorry. What kind of timeframe are we talking here?*"

"*About three minutes,*" he said.

I glanced at the others with surprise. "*And we'll be ready to attack?*"

"*No, I just meant to redo the one that just got messed up.*"

Why is it that every time I needed to have information in a hurry it took the longest to get it? Here I was getting ready to fight against Admiral Psycho and The Four Demon Batteries—it *did* have a ring to it—and my wizard in charge of dropping the demon battery supply was nitpicking.

"*I'm asking you when* all *of the runes will be ready, Warren,*" I said in a stern voice.

"*Oh, right. About twenty minutes.*"

"*That'd be perfect,*" I said with a nod to the others. "*Seems that our pal Reese is waiting for the moon to hit high noon, or whatever the equivalent is for roughly ten at night in the middle of the desert. Once that happens, he's planning on being fiendish.*"

"*The moon hits the apex in fifteen minutes,*" Warren replied soberly.

"*But Rachel and Jasmine—*"

"*Are basing their assumption on the power pulses they're feeling in the area,*" he interrupted. "*Unfortunately, those pulses are being inflated by the fact that there are demonic boosters in the area.*"

"Oh." I chewed gently on the inside of my lip while thinking things through. *"Wouldn't that mean they'd assume the moon would hit the apex sooner rather than later?"*

"No, but that's a good thought."

I felt a sense of pride at the compliment, seeing as how most of the time the mages considered me unlearned regarding their craft. It was a fair assessment on their part, but I'll take the little wins wherever I can get them.

"Thanks, I've been doing a little reading on the side—"

"The demons are pulling the power and storing it," Warren interrupted. *"What the mages are reading is a diminished scale of what's actually building up."*

I looked over at Rachel and Jasmine, who merely shrugged in response. A glance at Griff said that Warren's assessment made sense.

"So we need to attack him before that, right?" I asked.

"Only if you want to hit him before he's at full power," replied Warren.

"I think we'd probably like to do that." I sighed. *"Well, try and speed up your drawing, if you can."*

"One mistake will negate everything, Chief."

"Right." Of course it would. Why wouldn't it? We were about to face down a killer mage and a suite of demons, so being a few minutes off in the wrong direction was like icing on the cake. *"Okay, we'll do our best to be a thorn in Reese's side until you have everything ready."*

Chuck and Felicia had pulled back from the edges of the little building and started looking over their Desert Eagles.

I'd already checked and rechecked my mag about ten

times, but I still did it once more. I also ran an inventory over the ones hanging from my belt. Everything checked out.

It was go time.

CHAPTER 34

I took point, sneaking around the side of the building while staying low enough to keep the ventilation shafts for cover.

My initial thought was to stand up and start laying waste to them, but I had a better idea.

"Chuck and Felicia," I said, motioning them forward, "we've got three baby cannons with us. We can aim them all at Reese's head or we can aim two at Reese and one at the werewolf."

"What about the succubus?" Felicia said with a confused look.

"Hmmm?" I replied innocently as if I had forgotten about her.

"Freak," said Rachel from behind us.

"Maybe she's…" They were all giving me a sinister look. "Okay, okay, but I'm not shooting the succubus. I couldn't live with myself."

"I'll do it," said Chuck.

"I'll take out the mage," Felicia stated while still

shaking her head at me. "You get the werewolf, Chief. Not a fan of shooting one of my own, unless I have to."

Somehow *that* was okay, but me not wanting to blow away an incredibly attractive, well-muscled Amazonian succubus was a bad thing?

Whatever.

I nodded my agreement and set my sights on the werewolf. It wasn't much of a challenge considering they were all in a trance. Reese was the only one moving about and it was in a rhythmic fashion that Felicia would be able to compensate for without a fuss.

"Rachel," I said as I lowered my heart rate to keep the gun steady, "count us down."

"Three... Two... One..."

The bullets left their chambers within milliseconds of each other. Mine struck the werewolf right between the eyes, blowing his head apart like a melon. The succubus was falling backward as well, her head nothing more than a splat of what it once was.

Reese, though, was not hit.

The bullet that was coming his way stopped inches before striking him.

He turned around and plucked it out of the air, studying it for a moment. The look on his face was a mixture of confusion and amusement. I would have preferred full-on confusion or possibly terror.

"You may as well come out from behind the vents," he called out while spinning the bullet around in his hand. "It's not like they're going to give you much cover."

I fired at him again, just in case. The bullet stopped just as Felicia's had done. I aimed lower. It stopped, too.

"Honestly," Reese said in a chastising tone, "you're just wasting ammunition at this point."

I motioned for the others to stay put. There was no point in letting him know how many of us there were. He'd probably done enough of a calculation to know that there were at least three, but in his trance-like state, you never know.

I stood up.

"Ah," he said, smiling, though his eyebrows were both up. "It's you, Mr. Dex. I'm actually quite surprised. The explosion back at the morgue was quite powerful, after all."

"What can I say? I heal quickly."

"So it seems." He was all smiles, looking like Mr. Roarke welcoming a guest at *Fantasy Island*. "I suppose I should have expected an amalgamite to be tougher to kill than a standard supernatural." He shrugged. "Shame on me, I suppose. Not to worry, though. I shan't make the same mistake twice."

Keeping his eyes on me, he snapped his fingers and a bolt of energy split from his hand. It hit the fallen werewolf and succubus at the same time, covering them in a cocoon of light for a few moments. They weren't writhing about like I'd done when being smacked by one of Reese's electrical blasts, so I assumed this one was intended for healing.

Sure enough, the two creatures stood back up, looking as if they'd never been shot at all.

"Impressive," I admitted.

"Trivial," he replied. "I've got a nearly unlimited supply

of energy. Plus, I'm pretty decent with magic in the first place."

"Clearly."

"You, though," he said, wagging his finger at me while grinning playfully, "are somewhat of a thorn. How you were able to get through my magical shield the last time we met, and without any apparent effect to your person, was quite impressive."

I furrowed my brow at him. "Thanks?"

"Don't mention it. You see, that shouldn't be possible." He paced back and forth in front of his minions. "Anyone else would have been either bounced off my shield or they'd have been instantly killed." He looked up at me thoughtfully "That would depend on their level of power, you see?"

"Yeah, sure," I replied. Did he think I was an idiot? "Makes sense."

"But you went right through it like it was nothing, and that tells me something about you."

"That I'm special?"

"Clearly that, Mr. Dex." His expression was dull. "More importantly, though, it tells me that I could use someone like you in my army."

One thing I'd learned over the years was that bad guys always tried to get you on their side when you made them nervous. Mental manipulation was the only thing stronger than physical manipulation. Twist an arm and a guy will scream "uncle," but twist a mind and you'll get, "How may I serve thee, Great One?" I can't explain why my thoughts used Old English when thinking of dastardly things.

What I didn't understand was *what* he was afraid of. He'd kicked the shit out of me and my crew at the morgue already. So why would he be playing a game of get-me-on-his-side now?

Unfortunately, I didn't have much time to play along. The moon was reaching its apex and that meant even more trouble than we had now. It was time to misbehave.

"Gee," I said finally as I motioned my crew to join me, "it *does* sound like a hoot, Reese, but I'm afraid that your army's going to be gone before I've had the chance to enlist."

I had three mages with hands aglow and three agents with guns, leveled and ready to fire. It wasn't going to suffice to stop him, at least not without Warren's runes, but it may prove just enough of a pain in the ass to give us the extra time we needed.

"Very clever," he said with a disappointed shake of his head. "Sad, but clever." He then turned back to his pals and casually said, "Kill them."

CHAPTER 35

The top of the Excalibur became a light show for the ages. Fireballs and ice storms raged in a cacophony of magical malady.

Jasmine, Griff, and Rachel had their hands full throwing everything they could at Reese. He was easily defending them with his right hand while incessantly rebuilding the werewolf and succubus with his left. We peppered the two beasties with 50-caliber death, but they'd jump right back up within moments of falling.

"*Warren,*" I said through the connector, "*we could really use some help about now.*"

"*We can hear the racket up there,*" he called back.

"*Exactly, so hurry the fuck up!*"

"*I'm trying, I'm trying!*"

In the hopes that Reese's power consumption was impeding his ability to maintain his shield, I fired another bullet straight at him.

It dropped.

He rolled his eyes at me and then adjusted his hand to

launch a bolt of energy my way. I flew back far enough to smack into one of the vents. It didn't feel all that great, but at least I wasn't being encased in one of those sting-you-like-hell spells he'd thrown at me in the morgue.

Did that mean that Reese didn't have the bandwidth to fire one of those babies off right now? Were we giving him all he could handle?

Only one way to find out.

"Rachel, Jasmine, and Felicia," I said through the connector as I got to my feet, *"fire at the demons."*

Chuck and I kept sticking bullets into the heads of the two merged ubernaturals while Griff formed a shield of his own to protect the other mages.

It failed.

The bullets went through the demons as if fired at a wall of mist. The magic struck them, but the result was far worse than expected. They were somehow absorbing the energy, giving them even more power.

"Shit."

I didn't have to call off my mages. They caught the problem just as quickly as I did and turned their attention back to Reese.

"We seem to be at a stalemate," I called out to Reese.

"Not at all," he said with a smile. "I'm merely allowing your mages to fully exhaust their reserves before I negate them completely. Don't worry, though. Even after this little show of incorrigibleness on your part, I'll still leave the door open for you to join me."

"Seriously?"

"Merging someone like you with a demon would be quite a boon to my army, Mr. Dex."

"But you said I *can't* be merged," I noted.

"Under normal means, that's true." He cast two quick energy spells at Felicia and Chuck, knocking them away from firing while he healed his two minions. It looked like it took nothing out of him. "I did a little thinking about it after I thought you'd been killed. I thought it such a shame to have done you in so quickly. You see, my level of power *might* just be the thing that could allow you to merge." He put his hands out widely. "But since you're alive, you'd be a fantastic asset to my cause."

I needed to buy time for Warren to finish those runes, and I also had to make sure my mages didn't go fully depleted of energy. The moon was nearing its highest point in the sky, which sucked even more. While I had no clue what that would mean when fighting this bastard, my team had seemed pretty uneasy regarding the prospect. And we were already getting our butts handed to us... again.

"And you're sure that would work?" I asked, lowering my gun.

"I haven't a clue," he admitted with a shrug. "If it does, you'd be very powerful, indeed. If not, you'd die."

"Oh, well, sign me up, then."

He laughed at that. "You're going to die either way, Mr. Dex. Why not do it with the possibility of giving yourself more power than you've ever known?"

I nodded as if in thought, bringing my hand up to my chin. I'll be the first to admit that I wasn't much of an actor, but this guy's ego was so big that maybe it wouldn't take much to fool him. There'd only be one shot at it, though.

"How much longer, Warren?" I whispered, trying to keep my lips from moving.

"Two minutes."

"Everyone, listen up," I said while continuing my best ventriloquistic speaking, *"I'm going to motion you all to stop your attack in a second."* Rachel spun to look at me, but I gave her a glare. *"Do it when I say. No arguments, please. You all have to play along, no matter what happens."*

I lowered the gun a little farther and gave Reese a knowing look. "I see your point."

"Do you?"

"Everyone cease firing," I commanded while motioning my officers to stop their assault.

Griff kept the shield up until Reese halted his onslaught.

The hum of the vents was all that could be heard aside from the sound of vehicles below. All in all it made for a pleasant reprieve from the mayhem.

Keeping my eyes on Reese, I said, "If I do this, will you let my team go?"

"What are you doing, Chief?" said Chuck, who was obviously playing along.

I held up my hand to silence him.

"Sure, why not?" Reese answered my question with a careless nod. "It's not like they can beat me anyway. Besides, if my little plan works, they'll have to contend with me *and* you, and I'd frankly revel in watching you destroy your own team."

"Or you could include all of us in your plan," announced Rachel.

"That's not part of the deal," I said.

"Screw your deal," she replied with a little more drama than was warranted. "What's the point in trying to fight him? It's clear we're going to lose. You saw what he did to us at the morgue, and we're not even making a dent in his resources now." She scoffed. "And if you join him, we won't even last a minute."

"I'm in agreement," Griff said suddenly. His acting was actually quite good. "Honestly, I've grown weary of fighting two-bit criminals in this damn town." Griff *never* used foul language. "These last two nights have offered the most excitement I've had in years. It's been thrilling."

"What the hell is going on?" shrieked Chuck.

"Think it through," Griff replied, giving his partner a firm look. "We're wholly outmatched. Wouldn't you rather join the winning team than perish on an island of honor with the losing one?"

"But…"

"But nothing, Charles." Griff lowered the shield that was protecting the three mages. "We must face facts. Our lives have been shrouded behind a veil of boredom for years."

"I love how you talk," said Reese. "It's rather posh in comparison with the rest of the PPD squad."

Griff tilted his head. "I offer my thanks."

Reese crossed his arms and studied us all for a few seconds. I did everything I could to keep a look of genuine interest on my face. I even added a touch of forlorn to convey that I'd been defeated.

"You do realize," Reese said at a measured pace, "that if you're trying to pull a fast one on me, it won't work."

That's when Warren said, *"It's done"* through the connector. *"Want me to activate them?"*

"Hold for a moment," I whispered.

I dropped my gun and signaled Felicia and Chuck to do the same. Chuck kept the confused act going, but Felicia gently reached out and took the firearm from his hand and then set it on the ground along with hers.

"So you *are* being serious?" Reese said, still looking unconvinced.

It was my turn to shrug. "Maybe it's time to shake things up a little."

"Interesting," said Reese with a laugh.

"Warren," I said through a fake smile as the powerful mage clapped his hands, *"activate the fucking runes."*

CHAPTER 36

$\mathcal{I}$ crossed my arms and felt as much smugness as a person could manage. The mighty mage was about to have his power sources dropped back into oblivion, which would leave him as naught but a husk of the power he currently held.

"Something wrong?" said Reese, tilting his head. "You look like you are having a bout with gas."

"Huh?" I said, dropping my arms. "No, I just..." I coughed. Then through gritted teeth, I said, *"Warren?"*

"Sorry, Chief," Warren replied. *"Something went wrong. I'm trying to figure it out."*

"Super," I said while giving a crazy-eyed look at Rachel.

Reese wore a dubious expression. "Everything okay?"

"Yes, sorry." I clapped my hands and rubbed them together. "Just not an easy decision, you know. Plus, it doesn't look like my entire team wants to join in."

Reese shrugged. "Then they'll die."

"Right, I get that." Stalling for time wasn't all that difficult when you were dealing with an evil villain. They liked the drama, after all. "It's just that we've been friends for many years and that makes things a little tougher. I'd like a few moments to try and convince them."

A white light scanned across the top of the building the moment I finished my sentence. Reese and all of the demons, including the ones inhabiting the werewolf and succubus, flung their heads back and put their arms out in wide fashion.

My three mages followed suit.

It lasted all of thirty seconds, during which time everyone was silent.

"Warren," I hissed, *"what the hell is going on?"*

"He drew one of the items incorrectly, Ian," Serena answered for the wizard. *"I have him focused on redrawing it now. We will need another few moments. Please let him work so it can be done more quickly."*

"Fine," I said, not sure what to do. *"But all the mages and their demon friends just started glowing."*

"That means the moon has reached its apex," Serena explained. *"I've been studying alongside of Warren, so I've picked up a thing or two."*

"What exactly does the moon reaching its apex do again?"

"It restores full power to our mages, for one."

"Oh, well that's good."

"And it increased the power of any demonic possession."

"Oh, well that's bad."

I looked over at Reese's side of the playing field. The demon apparitions were definitely larger than they'd been a couple minutes ago.

Great.

It wasn't bad enough that we had an exceedingly

powerful egomaniac of a wizard with demon batteries giving him an unlimited supply of magic, now he was going to increase in power even more?

"*Wait a second,*" I said, thinking something was definitely amiss. "*The moon hits its apex every night and I don't see Rachel, Jasmine, and Griff doing this odd-looking light dance.*"

"*That's because our mages aren't in the vicinity of such power every night,*" she replied. "*Just like the runes Warren is currently in the process of perfecting, Reese's magical grid expands out from his demons.*"

I glanced up at that, looking around at the roof. Sure enough, there were pulsing lines of glowing white connecting to all three of my mages. They weren't as bright as the ones hitting Reese, but from the orgasmic look on Rachel's face—one I remembered quite well—it was clear she was being fed a good dose of energy.

"*Done,*" said Warren.

"*Done?*"

"*Yeah, Chief. It's all set. I had missed one of the glyphs on the thirty-third rune. You can't miss anything or it won't work. Now, if you—*"

"*Warren,*" I interrupted, "*if you don't activate those runes right now, I swear I'll come down there and punch you into next week.*"

"*Oh, right. They'll be up in about thirty seconds.*"

The moonlight event began to dissipate as Reese regained control of himself. He looked at me with glowing white eyes. It was kind of creepy.

I glanced over at Rachel, who was staggering slightly.

She looked at me with the same white eyes. It was kind of hot.

"All better?" I said to Reese.

"It's like nothing you've ever imagined," he said, looking somewhat blissful. "Soon, though, when we are taking over this world together, bending it to our rule, you will feel the immense joy of true moonlight."

"Sounds peachy," I replied with a smile.

"They're firing off in three seconds, Chief," said Warren through the connector.

My smugness returned.

"But there may be one teeny weeny problem with your plan, Reese."

CHAPTER 37

*R*eese's white eyes turned immediately dark as he realized that a set of runes had been flipped on. It dragged him and his two goons to the ground. The floating demons were writhing in pain. The ones inhabiting the werewolf and succubus must have been feeling similarly uncomfortable since they started clawing at themselves.

"What have you done?" said Reese, looking as though he was trying to catch his breath.

"Evening the playing field," I replied as I bent down to pick up the Eagle.

Unfortunately, I didn't get that far before the angry mage unleashed a massive bolt of energy, knocking me off my feet with such force that I fully expected there to be a hole in my chest.

It rang my bell pretty good, but this was no time for pain.

"*Get up,*" I commanded the rest of my team as I fought

to regain my footing. *"We have to stop him before he figures out how to undo the runes."*

Reese launched another volley my way, but I dived forward, getting under the streaming river of light.

I rolled back up to find Griff waving his hands in dramatic fashion. He replaced his shield as Jasmine and Rachel flung everything they had at Reese.

This time they *were* having an impact.

But the angry mage wasn't done yet. He put up a shield of his own and then sent a wave of power into the werewolf and succubus.

They pushed up to their feet and began running at me, Chuck, and Felicia. The beasties were moving faster than any beings—supernatural or not—should have been able to run.

I snapped up the Eagle and yelled, "Fire!"

There were times where you wanted to hear the cracking of gunfire. A banging sound that kicked you like a mule. Something that would give you the feeling of more strength as you took down the monsters that were coming at you. So it was a bit anticlimactic to see the bullets having their intended effect while making only tiny "pop pop" sounds. I would have to ask Turbo to supply a volume slider for moments such as these. Assuming we survived, obviously.

I knocked a decent-sized hole through the werewolf's chest and another took off half its head, but his initial momentum was enough to have him crash into me.

That should have been all there was to it. He should have been dead because Reese didn't have the bandwidth to heal him anymore.

But the thing was still moving. And not just wiggling about, either.

It sat up and started raining down blows, having me in full mount.

I put up my hands, fending off strike after strike. It reminded me of a UFC bout I saw at the Mandalay Bay Hotel a few weeks back.

"How the fuck are you still moving?" I yelled.

It was all I could do to stop the thing from pummeling me into dust. Fortunately, this is why cops always have someone watching their backs. Just as one crushing blow got through to my chin, Felicia slammed into the side of the creature, dislodging him from me.

I rolled over, feeling even more woozy than before. My chin was definitely going to bruise from that punch.

Felicia and the beast were wrestling on my one side and Chuck and the succubus were squaring off on the other.

They were both holding their own, but it was an impossible fight because these monsters had holes through their bodies and were missing half their heads.

Whatever those runes did that Warren fired off on the demons, it was currently backfiring with the werewolf and succubus. They were even more powerful than before, and bullets didn't seem to be much of a deterrent anymore.

In a nutshell, my team was still deep in the shit.

I glanced up to see if Reese was somehow animating them, but he was having enough of a struggle keeping my mages at bay.

That's when I noticed the demons behind Reese were no longer apparitions.

They were fully physical creatures now.

Green and scaled with red eyes, sharp teeth, and long claws. They were slender-built with a low center of gravity and their arms were long and lanky. There was little doubt that these things were going to be a bitch to kill.

"Are the demons gone?" asked Warren as if on cue.

"No, Warren," I said as calmly as I could manage while lifting up the Eagle and aiming it at one of them, *"they're really not."*

CHAPTER 38

*I*t had become abundantly clear that the Eagle was a useless instrument against the likes of a corporeal demon. Oh, it irritated the hell out of them—so to speak—but it didn't stop the things in the least.

This was a losing battle and I knew it.

It was time to use one of my special amalgamite skills. I was still discovering them all, but knew one that was fitting for this particular situation. I called it "Freeze."

I rarely did it because it made me rather cantankerous, I was exhausted for days afterward, and I lost some control over my emotions. But it gave me speed, healing, and power that was about the only weapon capable of holding these demons at bay.

The reason I dubbed it "Freeze" instead of something like "Rage," was because I became cold and calculating. Emotion essentially died. Besides, calling it something like "Hate" or "Rage" would draw comparisons to me being a normally mild-mannered scientist-type who turned big and green when he got ticked off.

"Everyone, listen up," I stated as the demons began heading toward me, *"I have to go into Freeze mode."*

"Oh goodie," said Rachel, having been around me in the past when I'd done things like this.

"Serena, you and Warren have to figure out some way to waste these demons. If that means you take me out at the same time, so be it. Don't let these fuckers survive. Are we clear?"

"We're clear," Serena replied in her business-like voice.

"Lydia," I called back to base, *"I'm about to go into Freeze. We've got demons and magic flying around us up here. If we don't succeed you're going to have to get the full council in on this."*

"Oh, honey, you can't—"

"Sorry, Lydia," I interrupted, *"but I have no choice. You may also want to get The Spin down here fast, but tell them to get the hell away even faster if this goes south."*

"Be careful, lover," she replied sadly.

"Keep them off me for as long as you can," I commanded the others before I closed my eyes and allowed the cold to set in.

The screams silenced, the flashing of lights grew dark, and my heart slowed to a crawl.

Entering the world of Freeze was something I could do quickly, but it was only used as a last resort. And it didn't last very long, so I had to be quick with my actions. Once I was fully engaged, assuming that Warren didn't kill me as collateral damage during his attack on the demons, I'd have to fight to control myself.

A small blue light began to grow out of the pitch black. Every strand of my being focused on it, building the deadness of emotion until only blue filled my vision.

My body was rocked by something hitting me. I assumed it was one of the demons or another blast of energy from Reese. But I felt no pain; I was already lost in the beginnings of the Freeze.

Now this wasn't some kind of berserker mode like Felicia was known to go into when her inner werewolf was too much for her to contain. It was more of a methodical destruction. I thought of it like a level of pain that gets so bad your brain stops you from feeling anything. I had to get deep enough into survival mode that I became grim, fierce, and dedicated to the eradication of anything that pissed me off.

My eyes snapped open.

A demon was on my chest, pulling back to rake its claws across my face.

I let it.

Then I reached up and grabbed it by the throat and snapped its neck with a flick of my hand.

The Freeze had begun.

CHAPTER 39

$\mathcal{T}$he demon didn't die. I hadn't done enough to warrant that. Plus, I understood that it would likely require a vat of that black goop from Warren to take the thing completely out. But it was disoriented enough to give me time to utilize it for a little destruction.

I stood and grabbed the demon by the arm and lifted it straight up. It struggled and slapped at me with its claws, but I didn't care.

Two of the others came rushing my way with fury in their eyes.

I already knew they weren't that fond of me, but they must have also realized that I had become their biggest threat at the moment.

I launched the demon I was holding straight into the incoming rush, knocking them down like a bowling ball does pins. They collapsed in a heap.

Turning, I saw that Chuck was struggling against the succubus. It was only a matter of time before she overpowered him. There was no emotion, per se, but rather just a deep-rooted understanding in my psyche that Chuck was on my team, which meant the succubus was not.

I sent a flying fist to what remained of her head. She flew off of Chuck and hit the ground, unmoving. I knew she'd get back up once the demon in her roused again, but that wasn't my problem right now.

"Thanks," said Chuck.

I looked at him impassively and then turned my attention back to the demons I'd bowled down. They were spreading out in front of me now instead of just running in. Obviously, they'd come up with a plan of attack.

The Desert Eagle was a few steps away, sitting between me and the demons. With a speed that would have seemed a blur to most, I jumped over and picked it up, checked the magazine, replaced it, and shot each of them before they had a chance to do anything. Then I turned and placed a shot through the werewolf that was attacking Felicia, and another through the succubus, who had started moving again.

This had given Felicia and Chuck enough time to get their weapons back in order. It wouldn't be sufficient for them, but it would help.

I could hear the chatter through the connector as my team yelled back and forth to each other. It was mostly noise, though, as my brain was in its own world. Their voices merely echoed in a cacophony of muddled sounds.

Even if I could have understood them, it wouldn't have broken my focus.

The demons needed to die.

Reese needed to die.

I glanced up at the mad mage who was continuing his battle with Rachel, Jasmine, and Griff. It was evident that I had to get to him and so I pushed forward.

This caught the attention of the angry demons. They already hated me because of their inability to possess my soul, and I'm certain that going into Freeze and making them look like waifs didn't help either. But now that I was moving to threaten their link to this world, they redoubled their efforts to stop me.

As one, including the werewolf and succubus, they attacked.

It wasn't like one of those shows where the kung fu artist stands there taking on fighter after fighter, one at a time. No, these guys jumped on me in a combined effort to take me out.

My bones were far denser than the average mortal, though, another product of my particular genetic make-up. Removing me from the equation was not going to be an easy task, especially when I was in Freeze. I'd still bleed, of course, but even then the Freeze would enhance my healing rate to nearly instant.

I couldn't last forever against them, though. Fortunately, I didn't need to. I just needed to keep them busy long enough for Warren to get the black goop on them.

I fought back at them ferociously, yet calmly. The feeling was strange. It was barely describable as "feeling" at all. If anything, it was as though I were nothing but a machine whose job was to demolish. An item comes into my world that is flagged as being on the destruction list and I crush it. There was no desire or hate, really. Just an emotionless requirement to destroy.

Every time I threw one of my attackers away, they'd surge back in.

Felicia and Chuck struggled to help, but the creatures were in a fit of madness that made it difficult. Still, every little bit helped. Had my mages been able to attack them with me, this would have gone much smoother, but they had to keep their focus on Reese. It was like playing chess. If you pressed your attack on one side of the board, your opponent would press back on another.

We were struggling against each other in a game of inches at this point.

That's when I heard the only voice that was ever able to get through to me during the Freeze. It was faint, but it broke into my mental blocks just enough so that I could hear it.

"Ian," said Rachel in what sounded like a whisper, *"Warren and Serena are constructing a void wall. When I say go, you will need to throw the demons through it."*

I couldn't respond to her, but I had enough presence of mind to search out the location of Warren and Serena. They were standing behind me, which placed the demons equidistant between Reese and them.

One of the demons stuck its claws in my neck. I grabbed its arm and bent it back with a sickening crunch. Then I snapped off each of its claws as it screamed in agony. This wasn't done out of malice, but rather out of self-preservation. The claws were dangerous and they had to go. So I removed them. Another punch to the face knocked it down as I drove my knee powerfully into the head of the one under me.

The succubus sent her whip across Chuck's back. He fell forward with a yelp as Felicia fired a 50-caliber round. It caught the succubus on the shoulder, blowing it apart.

"*Now, Ian,*" said Rachel desperately. "*Now!*"

CHAPTER 40

*A*s I said before, the Freeze didn't last forever, and I could feel my resolve starting to weaken. The more focus I had to expend, the quicker Freeze dissipated. And I was in a state of needle-like tunnel vision right now.

With a burst of energy that I knew was likely to knock me clear out of my hyper-focused state, I threw the leeching demons away and bolted toward the void.

Warren was waving his hands at me to veer away from the wall of black he'd created, but my safety wasn't as important as the destruction of these beasts.

At least this was what the part of my brain that was still in Freeze thought. Unfortunately, the part of me that was struggling to regain control considered self-sacrifice not nearly as appealing.

"You must," I said to myself.

"Fuck that," I replied to me.

Yes, I was quite literally talking to myself.

A demon slammed into me from behind. I fell and rolled with the blow, launching the demon through the air as I continued my somersault. It flew straight into the blackness and was no longer a threat.

The tip of my shoe hit the void as I came to a sliding stop. I yanked it back quickly and noted that it was gone. Fortunately, I wore my shoes a little loose; otherwise I'd have been short a toe at that moment.

"What the shit is that?" I shrieked.

"Your destiny," the frozen side of me replied without emotion.

I slapped myself and yelled, "Shut up!"

The whip of the succubus snapped around my neck an instant later, thankfully yanking me back from the wall of death. I doubted it was her intent to save me, but my ever-growing desire to live was rather pleased nonetheless.

I was starting to fatigue and Freeze was losing hold.

Thinking quickly, I pulled out the Eagle and fired it straight up at the succubus. It hit her in a not-so-friendly spot and she screamed a scream I'd likely have nightmares about.

Felicia kicked her in the back a moment later. The succubus was thrust forward far enough to allow Serena to step out and help her along the rest of the way into the void.

So much for that fantasy of being with an Amazon-sized succubus.

Two demons down, three to go.

"Everyone attack these goddamn demons," I yelled as inspiration struck and Freeze was nearly gone.

"But…"

"Everyone!"

They all turned their attention toward the demons. Reese did as well, but his intention was to heal them as fast as my crew attacked them.

But I had recalled something about my particular relationship with Reese. He couldn't block me out.

As my mages fired wave after wave of energy at the demons, and Chuck and Felicia supported their efforts by punching, kicking, and shooting the green-scaled things, I ran full force at Reese and launched myself at his mid-section, barely ducking a blast of energy.

We hit the ground and he began building up the same type of spell that he'd used on us at the morgue.

The tornado was coming again.

But this time I wasn't going to wait for it.

I pulled out the Eagle and fired it at point-blank range into his chest.

The growing noise faded, replaced by the screams of demons who were being systematically sent through the void.

"What have you done?" said Reese as his eyes dimmed.

"Stopped an asshole from taking over the world," I said through ragged breaths as I pushed up and leveled the Eagle at his head.

"You have no idea what you're doing." His voice was subdued and his breathing was gurgled. "Killing me will not stop us."

"Us?"

He began to chant as spittles of blood formed on his lips. His eyes started to brighten until there was a stream of light shooting from them.

Rachel hollered, "Kill him!"

This was enough to shake my mind back to the moment.

A 50-caliber bullet stopped Reese's chanting once and for all.

CHAPTER 41

I collapsed next to Reese's body as Rachel came over and lifted my head off the ground.

"Are you okay?" she asked.

"I've been better."

"You'll be out of it for a while, you know?"

I nodded.

The headache was already beginning. It always followed quickly behind the Freeze, or any of the other special skills I used. But I had to do it. We needed the time.

"I hate it when you do that," she said while running her fingers through my hair.

"It's the only way I can get you to touch me," I said, giving her a tired wink. "I'm feeling a lot of pain in my groin area, too, you know?"

"We're not allowed to play that game anymore, remember?" She smiled and shook her head. "Freak."

As if my head hadn't hurt bad enough, I heard the

growling voice of Paula Rose as she thumped across the roof.

"Great," I said. "I don't suppose you'd be willing to talk with her about—"

"Oh no," interrupted Rachel. "Fighting demons, werewolves, vampires, and evil overlords is one thing. There's nothing in my contract that says I have to tangle with your ex-girlfriends."

She helped me to my feet as Paula came up, wagging her finger at me.

"I've put up with a lot from you, Ian," she said. "*A lot.* But this crosses the line, even for you!"

I winced with each word. "Could you take it down a notch? I have a bit of a headache here."

"*You* have a headache?" She scoffed and looked around at everyone. Then she glanced down at the body of Reese and spun away. "Holy hell."

That was odd. She'd seen bodies before. Even ones that weren't all in one piece.

I looked down and noticed that Reese's corpse was transforming. He was turning green and scaly.

"Shit," I yelled, picking him up and running as best I could toward the void.

I had almost no energy left, but there was just enough adrenaline in me to launch his sorry ass at the black canvas.

Just as he passed through, his eyes flashed at me one last time.

Again, I collapsed.

"What the hell was that?" Paula said, clomping over toward me.

Fortunately, there was one person on my squad who had no issues going toe-to-toe with the CEO of The Spin.

"If you'll come with me," Serena said, taking Paula firmly by the arm, "I'll explain everything."

"But..."

Serena gave her a stern look. "Don't make me ask twice."

Paula wisely acquiesced.

CHAPTER 42

"And that's all he said?" asked Zack.

I was still suffering the post-effects of the Freeze, but the Directors insisted on being informed of the situation.

"Yes, sir," I answered tiredly.

"Do you know who the 'us' is in Reese's statement?"

"I have no idea, O," I replied to the mage. "My guess is that he meant the demon he was turning into before I sent him through Warren's void thing."

O nodded, along with Zack.

"Any casualties on the PPD side?" asked Silver.

"No deaths, sir. Just bumps and bruises. We'll be fine."

Zack leaned forward. "You *do* know how we feel about your using Freeze or any of your special skills, I hope?"

"I do," I said, "but when the fate of the world is at stake, you do what you have to do." I then rubbed my temples. "And believe me when I say I dislike going into Freeze far more than you do, sir."

Having a pounding headache was nothing compared to the pain from a Freeze. Imagine a migraine mixed with the worst hangover you've ever had. Then tack on an earache, light-sensitivity, and a general desire to kill anything that aggravates you. Or, as Rachel succinctly put it after I'd explained the symptoms to her, "So, PMS?"

"What is your plan now?" said Silver.

"Warren is doing more research into demonology. His goal is to build up his chops so he can be faster to the punch should this happen again." I took a sip of water. "The mages worked incredibly well together, but they've identified a few areas of improvement."

"What about your werewolf and vampire?"

"They…" I started, but rethought what I was about to say. "*We* are going to start working on our training again, sir. We've grown soft over the years because things have been too stable. While I'm not a fan of what Reese did, the effect of his actions was a wakeup call for the Paranormal Police Department."

"Indeed," agreed O. "EQK, have you any questions for Mr. Dex before we let him get some much needed rest?"

"Have you named your gun yet?" the pixie asked in his tinny voice.

I grinned. "Hadn't really thought about it, to be honest. I've just been referring to it as Eagle—"

EQK slapped his hand on the table lightly. "Lame."

"Does it really matter?" asked Zack.

"Of course, you mental fallacy!" EQK shot back. "How can you go around shooting dicks off with a weapon that has no name?"

"Hadn't thought of that, sir," I said as I took out the Eagle and looked it over. "Fine. I shall dub it, 'Boomy.'"

EQK clapped his hands and giggled some more. "That is so lame!"

CHAPTER 43

One of the only things that took the edge off these Freeze hangovers was a shot or two of whiskey.

"I'm going to head out," I said to Rachel as I stopped by her office.

"Three Angry Wives?" she asked, referring to the pub I stopped at from time to time.

I grinned at her, though it took some effort.

"Wanna join me?"

"I'd better not," she said. "You know what seeing you in Freeze does to me. Add in drinks and that spells trouble."

I liked trouble, but being with Rachel in such a way anymore was a no-no. "Trouble is bad."

"Yep." She then held up some papers. "Besides, I'm helping Warren go through some of these esoteric spells."

"No good?"

"Let's just say that I'm glad to have been born a mage and not a wizard." She dropped the papers back on her desk and looked up at me. "Get some rest."

"I will," I replied, nodding. "Don't stay too late."

I said my goodbyes to the others and drove down to the pub.

The bar was mostly full when I walked up and grabbed a seat, simultaneously indicating to the bartender that I wanted two shots.

They knew me.

"Mr. Dex?" said the voice of a man who looked to be in his early fifties.

He was fit with black hair that had splashes of gray mixed in, and he wore a suit that signaled he was well-to-do. Adjusting my focus a bit more, I sensed that he was a vampire.

"That's my name," I said before drinking down the first glass of whiskey. Then I said, "And you are?"

"Gabriel," he replied. "You may call me Gabe."

I eyed him again and nodded. Then I dropped the second shot of fire down my throat.

"What can I help you with, Gabe?"

"I believe it's me who can help you, Mr. Dex," he answered while standing up and gathering his things.

I turned toward him. "And how's that, exactly?"

"The mage who attacked your city today is just the first in a line who are coming." He pulled out a few twenties from his wallet and set them on the bar. "There will be *flashes* of more." He'd said the word "flashes" somewhat dramatically. "You will need to be prepared for them."

I wanted to ask him how he knew about this, but there was something about him that seemed familiar. There was also an air about him that said he knew what he was talking about.

"And you can prepare me?"

"No," said Gabe. "Only you can do that. I'm merely here to lend support when and where I can."

He started to walk out.

"And you plan to do that by leaving?" I called after him.

"I'll be around," he said over his shoulder. "Just keep your eyes open, Mr. Dex."

The door closed behind him and I turned and grunted at the bartender for another shot of liquid joy. She delivered it and I stared into the small pool of amber whiskey for a few moments.

Did I know someone named "Gabe" or "Gabriel?"

His face seemed so familiar, but that could have just been due to his being a vampire. Most of them were attractive, after all.

No, there was something more to it.

I just couldn't place it.

And what was with the "flashes" bit?

Finally, I shrugged and then drained the shot glass as the edge started coming off of my headache.

"Probably just some asshole," I whispered while rubbing my temples. "Probably just some asshole."

❧

The End

❧

Your bonus short story starts on the next page!

BONUS SHORT STORY: THE BLEEDING

J'd just graduated from basic training in the Netherworld Paranormal Police Department. My goal was to land a permanent position in the force, topside, preferably somewhere warm where I could use some of the trust money my parents had left me, but I'd take anywhere other than here.

Everyone in the Netherworld was either a vampire, a fae, a pixie, a werewolf, a mage, a wizard, a werebear... well, you get the idea.

I was none of them, and I was all of them.

I was what's known as an amalgamite, meaning that if you take all the races and put them together in a DNA soup, of sorts, you get me. No, I couldn't whip out my fangs whenever I wanted and I couldn't suddenly morph into doggie-mode during a full moon, but there were perks. In a nutshell, I was like a normal who had all the basic abilities of the various races. Speed, agility, strength, etc. I could even do basic magic, such as casting a tiny light when needed. I was also fortunate in that I healed very fast. Not that I was immortal, though the ladies did often refer to me as 'god' when we were having fun-time.

Since I wasn't a pureblood, I wasn't really a fit for the Netherworld. That sucked because the Netherworld was divvied up in factions.

Imagine a big city like New York. In the center, all of the races meld. They try to work together, get along, and see past their differences. It doesn't always work out that way, but it's better than the areas on the outskirts. That's where the different factions were. Think gangs, but with old money and old ways. If you were a fae in the fae area, you'd be about as safe as you could hope to be. Sure, there were still fae mugging fae and such, but it was pretty uncommon because the powers that be would seriously whoop the ass of anyone who attacked their own kind.

Now, if you were a pixie and you got too close to the fae area...well, it was nice knowing you.

It was really tough for a guy like me. I couldn't go into *any* of the areas because I wasn't pure enough for any of them.

Once I put on the PPD badge, though, I was teflon.

Anyone who even ruffled my freshly pressed shirt was looking at a few years in the slammer. If they did more than that, they'd get life with annual deep reintegrations. That meant they'd essentially go through mental reprogramming to the point where they weren't even close to who they once were. With some people, that wasn't necessarily a bad thing, obviously, but nobody wanted to lose their core personality.

"Let's cut down Merr Street, kid," said Sergeant Grumm, a veteran on the force who was tasked with mentoring me during my first year on the beat. He preferred to be called "Sarge," which was interesting due to the fact that he was a vampire. Most vampires were rather posh and particular, only wearing the finest clothes and eating at the finest restaurants, so having the desire to be called a working class name was peculiar. But Sarge was different than other vampires. He was the kind of guy who would rather eat a hot dog and have a beer than dine on fancy steaks while drinking wine. "Keep your eyes open. I got a feeling something's gonna happen today."

One thing I'd learned during my few weeks working with Sarge was that he had a knack for knowing when nefarious activities were afoot. It could probably be chalked up to experience, but his accuracy was a thing of legend.

"Guns?" I asked, reaching for my holster.

"Only if we've gotta," he replied in his gruff way.

Sarge wasn't a fan of using guns. In fact, I'd only seen him unholster his once since we started working together. As he put it, "Showing a gun makes people fear you. Any idiot can be tough while holding a gun. I'd rather people respect me for being the man I am. And if they don't, I'll beat that respect into 'em."

It was a difficult point to argue, but not everyone was Sarge. Most of us needed a weapon when facing down bad guys.

Me, for example. I was confident, but not like Sarge.

Maybe that had to do with the fact that my upbringing was dodgy at best.

I'd been raised topside by various families, moving from house to house and spending an equal amount of time in the orphanage. I was just too much of a handful for most normals. To be fair, nobody knew about my being an amalgamite until I'd hit my late teens, including me. Managing a kid like me when you're a normal is damn near impossible, and I'll admit that I was quite a handful. I still was, if I'm being honest.

Once the powers that be in the supernatural community figured out what was really going on, I got moved to the Netherworld. This was a grand experience for me seeing that I thought werebears and such were all bullshit. Turned out, they're as real as anything topside.

After a couple of years going through immersive integration, which was less than fun, I started finding my way.

That's when it became abundantly clear that the *only*

place I had a future in the Netherworld was as a cop. Again, being a one-of-a-kind in a world full of factions isn't fun.

Regardless, one day I was going to get topside. I had to because I knew I'd fit in well enough with the normals up there. It wouldn't be perfect, of course, but with my level of money it'd be damn close.

"Check it out, Sarge," I said, bumping his shoulder while pointing at a guy who'd clearly decided on wearing the wrong shirt that day. White was not a good choice when feeding on blood. "We've got a feeder."

I started to move, but Sarge put a hand on my shoulder.

"Take it slow, junior," he said. I hated it when he called me that. "Might be something, might be nothing."

"What do you think?"

"Oh, I think it's definitely something," he admitted, "but we got two ways of going about this: We can spook him and he'll run, or we can walk up to him and hope he plays nice."

I didn't have that same knack for sensing trouble like Sarge did, but I had a feeling that this guy was going to run.

Mr. Bloody looked up and locked eyes with me. Then he shifted his eyes to Sarge's. Finally, he glanced toward an alley.

"Shit," I said as the guy took off.

"Yep," agreed Sarge. "You chase him. I'll get the car."

CHAPTER 45

J bolted after Mr. Bloody, pushing past people while yelling for them to get out of the way. Most of them sidestepped me like good citizens, but others didn't budge until I hit them.

"Fuckin' cop!" yelled one guy I'd bowled over. "Watch where you're going!"

"Out of the way," I continued yelling as the chase went on.

One of the issues with the main city was that alleys were always full of people. This was because there were shops connected to most alleys, and quite a few of those connectors even had merchant stands along the walls.

Running a chase through the middle of the city was dicey at best.

The vampire was fast. This probably had to do with a desire *not* to get caught mixed with the fact that vampires were notoriously quick and agile. But I had the edge here because my genetics gave me those same enhancements, plus I got some perks from the other races, too, such as wolf speed and power. Fortunately, I *didn't* have the wolf disadvantage of needing to sniff and mark my territory.

So, I had the speed to catch Mr. Bloody, assuming I could circumvent the pedestrians getting in my way.

"Watch it, asshole," snarled one vampire after she hit the ground. "Damn half-breed!"

Technically, I was more than merely a half-breed, but I didn't have time to stop and explain that. She wouldn't have cared anyway. I wasn't a vampire, so to her I was akin to a piece of shit.

"Where are you, kid?" Sarge asked through the connector, a little device that was implanted in the brain of every PPD officer. It allowed us to communicate with each other hands-free. *"You got him yet?"*

"He just cut left on Corbel," I replied. *"Peds keep getting underfoot."*

"Knock 'em down," he said as if it were nothing.

"That's what I've been doing, but it still slows my progress."

"We'll get him, kid," Sarge said with a chuckle. *"Don't worry."*

Sarge had a very relaxed attitude about these things. I was more tense about it, but according to Sarge that was because I was still "pissing vinegar."

"Turned right on Miller," I called through the connector.

"Heading right toward me, then," Sarge replied. *"I'll get out here and we'll take him down."*

"Good. I'm closing in on him."

The vampire glanced back and saw that I was hot on his heels. He began pulling bodies into my path and even knocked over a cart.

Fucker.

Bad news for him was that he was so preoccupied with me that he didn't notice Sarge until it was too late.

Sarge may have been a bit saggy in the middle, but he wasn't a marshmallow.

He was older, slower, more relaxed, and he had a tendency of moseying instead of running. Hell, if he wore a cowboy hat and a set of suspenders, I'd go as far as to call him a good old boy.

But Sarge was also tough, street smart, and knew exactly where to punch someone in order to drop them on their ass.

That's exactly what he did to our vampire pal.

Take a runner who wasn't paying attention, mix that with the strength of a big man like Sarge who had a fist like a brick, and set them at odds. You'll end up with a mess.

That was the real reason Sarge didn't need a gun. He *was* a weapon.

By the time I caught up, the vampire was lying on the ground unconscious and Sarge was rubbing his knuckles. Tough or not, a punch like that had to hurt your hand.

"You all right?" I panted aloud, putting my hands on my knees while trying to catch my breath.

"Sure, I'm all right," he said, shaking his hand. "It'll be a cold day in hell before some pissant like this guy does any real damage to me, kid."

I nodded and then set about cuffing the vampire. It was easy since he was out cold, but when he came to he started wriggling around with a vengeance.

"Let me up, fuckers," the guy growled.

"We'd be happy to do it," Sarge replied, snapping his

fingers at me and pointing at the guy. "By 'we' I mean Officer Dex here."

I pulled Mr. Bloody to his feet and started pushing him toward the car.

Time to book him.

CHAPTER 46

*W*e dropped off Mr. Bloody and headed back on the road, but I gave instructions to have the blood on his shirt tested. Sarge and I both had a feeling that it wasn't going to turn up belonging to cattle. It'd be more likely a werewolf or a fae.

"Sarge," I said as we cruised down Main, "how do you always know where these guys are going to be coming out?"

"What do you mean?"

"The guy we just chased," I replied. "I know I was giving you his play-by-play as I ran after him, but he could have easily taken two more turns before getting to you."

He was nodding slowly.

"Experience, I guess," he answered finally. "When you've been on the force as long as I have, you start getting a sixth sense about these things, junior. Like a learned intuition." We turned on Draper. "You'll get it eventually, if you live long enough."

"Nice."

"I'm not joking here," he said seriously after we stopped at a light. "The fact is that you're still young. Most cops your age are a little too eager and they end up on the dead end of a fight." The light turned green and he continued his leisurely pace down Draper. "Nothing you can do about it other than hope you're one of the lucky ones. I nearly lost my ass more times than I can count when I was your age. Goes with the territory."

That was probably true, but it wasn't something I liked hearing. Maybe I *was* a little too anxious to get into the mix of things, but when you had this much power floating around in your system it wasn't exactly easy to shut it off. Even though Sarge was a supernatural, he wasn't built like me.

But I got his point.

Mostly.

"It's just that you always seem so laid back and you still catch the bad guy," I laughed. "It's not that easy for me."

"Yep," he agreed. "It's the way of things, kid. You'll get better, just need some seasoning."

If I had a dollar for every time I'd heard that sage advice from one of the older cops over the last few months, I'd be able to buy a pretty nice bottle of wine. At some point, assuming I made it to the ripe age Sarge had attained, I was going to get a junior cop of my own. When that happened, I'd remember these discussions and try my damndest to give concrete suggestions instead of 'wisdom.'

"Let me tell you a story, kid," Sarge said after a connector dispatch call came in that was covered by another set of officers. "There were these two bulls standing on top of a hill, see? One of them was young and the other was older and experienced."

"I take it the two bulls represent us?" I asked.

He glanced over at me. "You wanna hear the story or not?"

"Sorry."

"Anyway," he continued, "one day the rancher showed up and unloaded a bunch of new cows. They were a fine looking bunch, too. Well, the young bull got all excited and yelled out to the older bull, saying, 'Look at all them new ladies down there. Let's run down and fuck one!' The older bull stepped in the younger bull's way before he could take off, and mentored him, saying, 'Why don't we *walk* down there and fuck 'em all?'"

Okay, so I laughed at that, but I also got his message.

I think.

"Patience is a virtue," I remarked. "I got it. But it's difficult to remember that when you have a perp taking off through the alleys."

"Sure is," Sarge admitted. "Still, I'd argue it's better to take your time and get your sights set than to rush in and find you've been ambushed."

Ambushed was not a word cops liked to hear.

One of the many tough things about being a rookie in the Netherworld PPD was that I didn't have the patience to wait to learn all the things I needed to learn in order to have patience! Catch-22, I suppose.

"You know," I said, turning in my seat, "I heard another bull story that's equally important, though it has a different meaning."

Sarge cracked a smile. "I'm listening."

"There were three bulls standing atop a hill talking about a new bull who was due to arrive. The three who were having a conversation already had their hierarchy set. There was a large one, a medium one, and a small one." I cleared my throat. "The large bull stared firmly ahead and declared, 'I sure hope this new bull doesn't expect me to share any of my cows, 'cause that's not going to happen.' The medium bull snorted once and announced, 'I may not be as big as you, but I'm not giving my cows up either.' The smallest bull squeaked, 'I know I'm nowhere near the size of you guys, but I only have one cow at this point. I can't afford to give her up!'"

I could see the anticipation on Sarge's face. He always seemed to love these little jokes. If he didn't have one to share, he was looking for one he could store in his memory for later.

"Anyway," I went on, "the rancher showed up and let the new bull out of the trailer. The thing was huge, dwarfing even the largest of the three bulls on top of the hill."

"That ain't good," Sarge chuckled.

"Well, the big bull changed his tune a little, saying, 'I suppose I don't need *that* many cows in my stable.' The medium bull agreed, saying, 'Most of my cows nag at me all the time anyway. I could stand to let a few of them go.' But the small bull did something unexpected. He lowered his head menacingly at the new bull. Then he started pawing the ground angrily while snorting."

"Oh, shit," bellowed Sarge.

"'Are you insane?' asked the big bull with wide eyes. 'He'll rip you to shreds.' The medium bull looked equally shocked. 'That beast down there will annihilate you.' But the small bull kept his fierce stare straight ahead and whimpered, 'I just want to make sure he knows I'm a bull!'"

Sarge released one of his trademark belly laughs as we pulled up at the next light.

Whenever I could get Sarge to howl with laughter, it was going to be a good night. Whenever Sarge started getting too serious, that meant the night was going to drag on.

Dispatch called through a global connection. *"We've got a disturbance at The Stipend on 3rd."*

"Officer Grumm here," Sarge replied, still giggling. *"We're only a few blocks out. We'll take it."*

"Assigned."

The Stipend was a bar known for tussles. If there wasn't a fight there at least twice a week, that meant something naughty was being planned. The factions that frequented the place rarely worked together, but when they did it was often far worse than when they just battled each other.

"Bar fight," I sighed, having at least learned that much during my limited experience.

"Yep." Sarge flipped on the lights. "Still want to go topside and miss all the action down here, junior?"

"Most definitely," I answered without hesitation. "I don't have any safe zones in the Netherworld, Sarge. You know that."

He sniffed. "Not likely to have any up there, either."

"True, but I have money up there, so I can afford some solace."

Sarge didn't respond to that and I kind of felt douchey for bringing it up. He wasn't one of those vampires who was loaded, after all. At least he hadn't mentioned anything about it, and he *never* did anything extravagant. My guess was that he was putting in his time on the force so he could get a pension and pick up a nice, quiet place somewhere in the valley, away from the hubbub of the city.

"Only time I've been topside was during a Retrieval call for one of my repeat offenders," Sarge said as we pulled in front of The Stipend. "Was considering trying out for the Retriever Training Program at the time." He grunted and stepped out of the car, coming to my side. "Bad idea."

"Trying out for the Retrievers, or going topside?"

"Yep."

CHAPTER 47

*W*e walked into The Stipend to find that things hadn't gotten out of control yet. That happened now and then. We'd get a call from Chip, the owner, because he knew when things were going to escalate, but when we arrived it would still be at a simmer. Better that than there being a full-out brawl in the works.

"Chip," Sarge said in greeting.

"Hey, Sarge," Chip replied in his skittish way.

Chip was not what you might call an imposing figure. He was rail thin, had a sunken face, stringy brown hair, and he was just *too* nice. Everyone was "right" in Chip's mind. Of course, he also advocated handing out trophies to those who landed in last place at sporting events. To be fair to Chip, that was likely the only way he'd ever get a trophy.

"What do we got here?" Sarge asked.

It was obvious what we were dealing with, though.

There was a group of werebears sitting on the left side

of the place and a group of fae sitting on the right. While there wasn't a physical line separating the two, the imaginary line was damn near visible.

The bears weren't in full form or anything, but it only took a spark to go from dark stares to battle.

I took a quick glance around and found tiny groups of other factions hiding in the shadows. It made zero sense to me why they were even stupid enough to stay in here. Then again, small groups didn't tend to get messed with as much as larger groups. They'd get picked on a bit, but it wasn't worth the fight. It was only when you had two decent-sized gatherings that the shit really hit the fan.

"Bears and fae this time," Chip said, keeping his voice low.

Sarge already knew that the moment we'd walked in, but by asking the question aloud it made the two sides consider the situation more logically. Nobody wanted to go to jail, after all, especially if it ended with you stuck in reintegration.

"How do you want to handle this, Sarge?" I asked.

He pulled up a bar stool and took a seat, making all the grunts and such that went along with being a man of his age.

"Best way I can see is for me to have a cranberry juice while you head over there and have a conversation with those fine people."

"Cranberry juice?" Chip asked.

"I'm on duty, Chip."

"Ah, right."

I truly had no desire to stand between a bunch of bears and fae, but every time I handled a new situation like this,

Sarge gave me points. Assuming I didn't fuck it up, of course. When I got points, that put me closer to getting full-cop status, and that meant I was closer to getting topside.

"Any words of wisdom before I go over there?" I asked.

"Don't piss 'em off," Sarge replied while holding up his drink in salute.

"Thanks."

After taking a deep breath and remembering that my uniform and badge were there to help protect me from being annihilated, I put on an air of confidence and sauntered over.

All eyes turned to watch me.

I grabbed a chair and spun it around so I was sitting on it with my hands on the backrest.

"How are you all doing on this fine evening?" I asked.

"What do you want, half-breed?" snarled one of the bears.

I wanted to explain my genetics, but it just didn't seem like the right purview.

"Oh, I'm just here to make sure everyone is having a good time," I answered smoothly. "The last thing anyone wants is for there to be a fight. That would ruin an otherwise lovely evening, wouldn't you say?"

There was no response.

"Yep," I continued, "a clear night like this would be a shame to miss due to being in jail."

The werebear who spoke out at me winced at that comment. Then he leaned back and crossed his arms.

"There ain't gonna be no fight," he said finally.

I smiled. "That's good, then."

"Fae ain't that stupid," he added, turning his eyes toward one of the fae.

I stopped smiling.

"And bears aren't that smart," replied a fae who was seated close to me.

I raised an eyebrow at the fae, thinking that her comment made no sense at all. Why would it be *smart* for the bears to fight the fae? Was I missing something here?

"Huh?" said the werebear before I could.

"See?" replied the fae.

"Nope," I answered.

"Ah, that's right," she said with a sly look. "You're an amalgamite." It was said as if she'd just thrown up a little in her mouth. "So you're dumb, too."

"I'm not dumb, you fu..." I stopped myself, getting what she was doing. "You're trying to goad me and my werebear friends into a first strike so you can claim you were only acting in self-defense. Smart."

"I know."

"We're *not* your friends, half-breed," the bear pointed out. "We'd rather befriend these fucking fae than you."

I frowned at him. "Nice."

It was obvious that playing peacemaker wasn't going to work, so I was going to have to get tough. When Sarge did this, it worked. When I did it...usually not.

But I had to try and use the same tactics that Sarge employed. If I didn't, the question would arise about my following his teachings. I wasn't a fan of those lectures.

"All right," I said, standing up and putting the chair back, "listen up. I don't want to have to call for backup, but I damn sure will if it comes to that. So," I instructed, pointing at the werebears, "you're all going to leave the building out the east door." I then pointed at the fae. "And you're going out the west. Neither of you are going to cut around to start any trouble, either." I gave a firm glare. "Are we clear?"

"Nope," said the werebear as he stood up from his chair and began shaking out his limbs. "I ain't had a good reintegration in a few years. They sting a little, but they're also usually worth it."

"What are you saying?" asked the fae.

"That I'm looking for a fight, you stupid ass." He then gave her a nefarious grin. "Unless you and your fae pussies are too afraid, of course."

In response, the fae stood up.

"Come on, guys," I called out, putting my hand out to stay both sides, "it's really not worth it."

As one, the bears all started morphing.

"Sarge?" I bellowed. "Could I get a little help here?"

"You're doing fine, junior," he called back. "Might want to back away from them a little, though."

A collection of roars sounded and I dived to the ground.

CHAPTER 48

*T*he only thing that saved my hide from being torn to shreds was that each side was too focused on whooping each other's asses.

You would have thought that a fae would have no chance against a werebear in full form, but fae are super fast and very tricky. For every haymaker punch that a bear threw, the fae would duck, land two or three punches of their own, and jump away. Then they'd fake an attack, which only caused another unbalanced, slow swing to extend from the bear.

But soon the bears tired of this game and just lunged after the fae, crushing them to the ground and raising up menacing paws to swipe away at their fallen foes.

I cannoned into one of the bears that was incredibly close to ripping the throat out of a particular fae. My attempted tackle didn't quite knock the bear over. In fact, it felt as though I'd tried to knock over a concrete wall, but it sufficed enough to make him miss the fae by about a half-inch.

In response, the fae punched *me* in the ribs and then kicked *me* away.

"What the hell?" I yelled at her, holding my ribs.

"I don't need your help, you fucking amalgamite!"

The bear then backhanded me and sent me flying into a table. If I were a normal, my hip would have been decimated by the collision.

"Thanks," the bear said to the fae, before pulling its paw back for another swing.

"No problem," replied the fae. Then she brought up her knee into the bear's groin, saying, "This is going to hurt."

It must have, too, considering the howl that the bear unleashed.

But now the fae was on top and she had pulled out a knife. It wasn't one of those little knives you see on TV when chefs are carving carrots into amazing floral garnishes, either. Yes, I watched those shows. The blade she wielded was long, with a hooked top and a black handle.

Just as she was about to drive it home, I pulled out my gun and shot her hand.

She shrieked and dropped the knife.

It landed point-first on the bear's leg, sinking in about an inch.

He howled in pain and slapped the knife away.

"You shot me!" yelled the fae, turning at me threateningly. "I'll fucking kill you for that."

The sound of gunfire had grabbed the attention of everyone else in the room, too. As one, they got up from their individual battles and glared at me.

Great.

By discharging my firearm, I'd succeeded in giving them a common enemy.

CHAPTER 49

*T*here were a few options for me at that point, with the most obvious being to curl up in the fetal position and wait for the world to go dark.

I could shoot at them, but I'd end up getting written up for doing that. It was one thing to shoot the hand of a fae in order to protect the life of a werebear, but dispensing my firearm into a bunch of these guys would be frowned upon.

"I've got backup coming, junior," Sarge called out between sips. "Might be a good time to put your gun down."

I glanced at the gun and then back up at the snarling faces who were bent on destroying me.

With a sheepish smile, I reached back and set the gun on the bar.

My hope was that they'd back off, but it didn't look like that was going to be the case. They weren't likely to kill me, but they did seem to be wearing faces that indicated they meant to do me harm.

So much for a badge and uniform.

"Uh…Sarge?"

"You got all them special skills, kid," he said. "Use one of them."

That was my other option. Or, more accurately, options. Over the course of my life as an amalgamite, I'd learned that I had some special skills. I could use *Freeze* to deaden my emotions, turning me into a fighting machine. There was *Haste*, which made me super fast, but still allowed me to control the amount of damage I was inflicting at any given time. *Superbone* was one that was only intended for loving the ladies. A quick glance at the fae I'd shot made me consider using that one, but I doubted she'd be consenting at the moment and I wasn't the type of guy who acted without consent. Besides, the last time I'd employed *Superbone*, I'd ended up in the hospital alongside the poor succubus who'd been on the receiving end of it. Think about those little blue pills and the "seek medical attention if you have an erection lasting more than four hours" warning. Mine was more than four hours. No fun. For a time I could use one I called *Flame*. It made anything I touched turn super hot for a couple of minutes. This was great in high school when a bunch of kids tried to gang up on me. I'd just go into a classroom, summon *Flame*, touch the doorknob, and smile as some of the dumber ones yelped while trying to open the door.

The only option that made sense in this circumstance was *Haste*.

But I couldn't just flip a switch. I needed a few seconds to calm my mind and prepare.

"I need about thirty seconds to do any of those, Sarge."

He sighed and got up.

"All right, you lot," he called out. "How many of you intend on going to jail tonight?"

They all raised their hands.

"That many," he mused, grunting. "You do realize that you'll get full integration if you lay a hand on my partner here, right?"

The bear growled. "He used a weapon."

"To save your mangy hide," Sarge noted in a patronizing tone. "Best you not forget that. You'd be dead right now, if it weren't for him."

"Don't talk down to me, old man," the bear warned.

I was too involved in controlling my thoughts to look up at Sarge, but I knew he was giving that bear a dark look. There was something about the way Sarge stared down perps that was unteachable.

"Son," he said in such a way that made the hairs on my neck stand on end, "you may want to curb your attitude when speaking to me."

"Oh, sorry, I was..." The bear stopped and then blurted, "Fuck you, you geriatric fucker!"

"*Ready yet?*" asked Sarge.

My mind was set.

I summoned *Haste*.

"*Yep.*"

The world slowed to a crawl. I could see eyes blinking at half speed, pulses throbbing in their necks, and even the tiniest movement of hair caused by the air conditioning duct. But I didn't have time to dawdle. *Haste* wouldn't last forever and when it died, I'd be exhausted.

I moved in and landed a perfect right against the fae's chin, knocking her on her ass, out cold.

Stepping past her, I kicked out and connected with the underside of the bear's jaw. He hit the ground, too. When you knew where to kick a bear and you actually had time to successfully place that kick, it didn't hurt your foot so bad.

Once those two were down, the others started to move. This happened so slowly that it didn't bother me in the slightest. Nobody in this bunch had a chance against me at the moment.

And so I became a maelstrom of pain.

I kicked, punched, elbowed, flipped, and stomped.

Within a minute, the only two left standing were me and Sarge.

The bears and fae were either unconscious or wondering what the hell hit them. One thing was for sure, they were all concussed. I made sure of that. Headaches were most definitely in their futures.

Of course, there was a headache waiting for me, too. As soon as *Haste* wore off, I was going to feel like I was having the worst hangover ever. Sometimes they could be mitigated if I was able to get my hands on energy elixir. But that wasn't going to happen here. I *could* drown the pain with whiskey, too...if I weren't on duty. There was no apparent reason for why this happened, other than my brain trying to reconcile the fact that the world just went incredibly fast and then slowed back to a crawl. Well, not a crawl, but it sure felt that way compared to the speed of *Haste*. I would imagine it'd be like hitting high G-Forces and then instantly stopping.

With nobody else to fight, I released *Haste*.

My brain throbbed in response, and I staggered.

Sarge walked over and helped me navigate through the fallen bodies. He got me to a chair and I sat down, holding my head in my hands. Honestly, I felt a bit envious of the fallen fae and bears at this moment. A concussion was nothing compared to this.

"That's some damn fine skill you've got there, junior," Sarge said, slapping me on the back. Ouch. "You've been telling me since we got paired up that you could do some interesting things, but this takes the cake."

I looked up at him with a wince. "Could you lower your voice just a little, Sarge?"

"Ah," he whispered. "Sorry. Didn't know it gave you a headache to do this."

"Horrible headache."

"Aspirin help?"

"No," I answered. "Either need to sleep or get some energy elixir." I left out the bit about the whiskey.

"Got two shots of energy in the car," Sarge replied as a bunch of cops poured into The Stipend.

"Seriously?"

"It ain't standard carry," he explained while helping me to my feet, "but sometimes you need what you need to do this job. Got healing and strength in there, too."

The other officers set about cuffing the bears and fae as Sarge dragged me outside.

"*Officers Grumm and Dex,*" said a voice through the Connector, "*your blood check on the vampire came back in. It's not cattle.*"

"*Had a feeling,*" replied Sarge. "*Didn't smell right.*"

"What is it?" I asked after downing the energy shot. It cleared my head almost immediately. *"I'm guessing werewolf."*

"Human," came the sobering response. *"It's from a normal."*

"How's that possible?" I asked, slack-jawed, while staring at Sarge.

"Damn if I know," Sarge replied, *"but we're going to sure as hell find out."*

CHAPTER 50

My head had fully recovered and I was feeling pretty decent. The elixir would wear off eventually and then I'd need sleep, but for now I was feeling quite nice.

Sarge was driving us toward the vampire area in the Netherworld. It was clearly the most sensible place to investigate, if for no other reason than to see what they might know about the perp we caught with a normal's blood on him. But I sure hated having to go to the outer edges of the city.

"I was thinking I'd just stay in the car, Sarge," I said off-handedly. "Do a little research."

"That's not happening, junior," he replied, grinning. "You'll be fine. Just let me do the talking." He turned onto Lakos and pulled up to a large set of iron gates. "Besides, you'll be doing this on your own at some point."

"Not if I can get topside."

He shook his head at me as a vampire guard approached the car from the opposite side.

"Ain't any better up there, kid."

I didn't respond. He couldn't see my point of view any more than I could see his. Even though he was a cop, he *could* find solace in the area we were about to enter. I had nowhere to go. Plus, I'd spent the majority of my life topside. I already knew what it was like.

Sarge lowered his window and showed his badge to the guard. Technically, he didn't need to do that. He was a vampire, after all. But it was clear he wanted it known that we were on official business.

"Need to see the council," he explained.

"Council won't meet with that one," the guard replied, motioning toward me. "He can stay out here."

"I'm all for that," I mumbled.

Sarge flipped his data pad on with a sigh. Then he spun it around to show the guard.

"We've got a warrant, pal," he stated. "Now, open the damn gate and tell the council to be in chambers or there'll be hell to pay."

The guard sneered at Sarge and then gave me a scornful look. He walked back around the car and into the little booth he'd been in when we'd arrived. He picked up a phone and nodded a few times, clearly informing the council of our situation.

Finally, the gate opened and we drove in.

I pointed up to the left, drawing Sarge's eye away from the fact that I was giving the guard the finger.

"What?"

"Nothing," I replied, feeling self-satisfied. "Thought I saw something."

He squinted over at me for a moment but didn't comment.

It probably wasn't the greatest idea for me to rile up anyone in this community, but sometimes it was nice to be on the superior side. The warrant gave me that. It was fleeting, sure, but I'd take it.

We arrived at the council building.

The place looked more like a 5-star resort, but that was the way with vampires. They didn't do things tamely. They also didn't do things modern. The place *was* gorgeous but in that Dracula's castle style. Spires, stained glass windows, dark stone work...all of it straight out of a movie. Actually, it was more likely that the movie was reflective of this joint.

At least it wasn't situated atop a hill that was accessed via a long and winding road.

"Again," Sarge said, giving me a sharp look, "I'll do the talking." Then he put his hand on my shoulder. "And no hand gestures."

"You saw that?" I asked, shocked.

"No," he replied, "but I had a hunch."

Oops.

I followed Sarge up the steps to the front door. Two female guards stood there, blocking our way. As Sarge went over the warrant with the one, I stood there eyeing the other.

They were both incredibly attractive. That wasn't surprising, most vampires were. Well, maybe not Sarge, but he wasn't one to play to the innate pompous nature his people shared.

"Do you have an eye problem?" asked the guard I was cradling with my stare.

"I do, in fact," I replied seriously. "Seems that something has entered my vision that I just can't shake."

She tilted her head at me.

"Ever been with an amalgamite before?" I asked, leaning in. "I can take you places you've never been."

"Like the gutter?" she challenged.

"If that's what you're into," I replied with a shrug.

Her face turned sour at that. Okay, so not my best line, but sex was a jousting session as far as I was concerned. I didn't mean that in a tawdry way. Okay, maybe I did, but the point was that it was rare to walk into a bar, head up to a super-hot chick, simply say, "So….wanna fuck?" and get a positive answer. That method *had* worked before, believe it or not, but I tended to get slapped more often than I got laid.

I couldn't help but try, though. I had a reputation for having quite the libido.

It was a blessing and a curse, though it was soon to become more of both. This was due to the upgrades PPD officers got when they became full cops. It would mean that each of my genetic slices was going to get a boost. In and of itself, that wasn't a bad thing. What concerned me was the fact that each of those boosts caused a horniness point to be added to your system. So, if you were a mage, you'd become better with magic *and* you'd be hornier than usual. Vampires became more agile and hornier. And so on. Since I had facets in my DNA from every race, I'd be boosted in everything. In other words, I was going to get a bunch of horny points. If what folks said was true, I'd end up as the horniest dude in both the Netherworld and topside.

"Anyway," I said as Sarge seemed to be wrapping things up, "I can do things to you that a regular vampire couldn't."

"Like make me vomit?" she countered.

I almost went with that "If that's what you're into" line again, but...no.

"Your loss," I said with a sad smile. "I guess multiple orgasms aren't a draw for you?"

"Yours or mine?"

I smiled wryly. "Both?"

"Come on, junior," Sarge called over to me. "We've got work to do."

I whipped out my police card and handed it over to her.

"Just in case," I said, giving her a wink.

She crumbled it up and dropped it into the trashcan next to her.

"I'd rather fuck a pixie."

CHAPTER 51

The inside of the building was opulent. Full of antiques and large fabric draperies. The foyer was awash with marble floors and stonework walls, all tied together with deep-red wood furnishings.

We walked into the council room and found three representatives waiting for us. Two women and one man. All older with slicked-back hair and drawn faces.

None of them looked at me, negatively or otherwise.

It was as though I didn't exist.

Fucking snobs.

"Bertram Grumm," said the woman seated in the center, "it's been a long time."

"Bertram?" I chuckled out of the corner of my mouth. He glared in response. "Sorry."

"Maybell," he replied with a nod, looking back at her.

"Maybell?" I whispered to myself, not wanting to get in trouble again.

These *were* old vampires.

"What brings you to the council today?" she asked,

signaling that the pleasantries were through. "I trust it's important, seeing that you have a warrant."

"It is," Sarge answered while glancing down at his data pad. "Picked up a kid by the name of Rick Eaves. Vampire. Had blood all over him."

"A battle with a werewolf wouldn't require a warrant," spat the snide little vampire next to Maybell.

"No, it wouldn't, Ramesses," Sarge agreed.

Ramesses? Come on!

"Well, then?" pressed Ramesses.

"This kid had the blood of a normal on him."

The council all looked at each other in shock. They were either good at acting or they were honestly surprised to hear this news.

"Where did you find him?" Maybell asked.

"City center. Junior here chased him down."

None of them even glanced my way. I desperately wanted to start making faces at them, but I had the feeling that Sarge would just get pissed. It wasn't easy to hold back, though. I hated pretentious douche cabbages like these pricks.

Maybell cleared her throat, looking somewhat uncomfortable. "What would you ask of us?"

"Do you know the kid in question?" Sarge asked.

They looked at each other.

"No," she replied, "but it's not like we know every vampire out there."

"Of course," remarked Sarge. "And I don't suppose you've heard of anyone getting their hands on some fresh meat from topside down here?"

"Absolutely not," Maybell replied as if slapped. "And

the insinuation that we would even consider such a thing is insulting."

Sarge wasn't bothered by that. It took a lot to ruffle his feathers. His was a mind that stayed calm in most any storm.

"No offense was intended," he replied without inflection. "I'm assuming you won't mind us looking around?"

"*You* may," Ramesses said, "but not your half-breed boy there."

"I'm not a fuc—"

Sarge put up his hand to stop me before I said anything too insulting.

"He's a police officer, Ramesses. Whether you are a fan of his particular genome or not is irrelevant." He held up his data pad. "This warrant allows him here. It allows us *both* to be here and to search all we want. I was merely trying to be polite."

Ramesses crossed his arms in response.

"You may search the area as you see fit, of course," Maybell said in a voice that was suddenly sweet. Too sweet. "And your amalgamite may join you, as well. I shall inform the guards to allow you both safe passage."

"Thank you," Sarge said with a slight bow.

I didn't know if I should bow also, but I refrained. There was no point in looking the fool. Then again, maybe it was rude that I *didn't* bow. I don't know. Fact was that I didn't feel she deserved the respect. None of them did. They were all just a bunch of self-righteous, racist shitheads in my book.

"*Let's go,*" Sarge said through a direct connection. "*My gut says that was too easy.*"

"*Agreed.*"

"*There's definitely something going on.*"

"*Yep.*"

"*And they're not going to make figuring it out easy.*"

"*Nope.*"

"*Thanks for the gripping discourse, junior.*"

"*Any time.*"

CHAPTER 52

The area was clean. At least the spots we could see. It wasn't like we were talking a small amount of space here.

Each faction had a ton of buildings, open land, suburban spots, etc., so finding a few humans here was akin to finding a pixie who loved goblins.

"They could be hiding anywhere, Sarge," I whispered as we headed back to the car.

"*Use your connector,*" he replied. "*No arguing that something...*" Sarge stopped and put out his hand. "Did you hear that?" he said aloud.

"Hear what?"

"I could have sworn I heard a..." He stopped again, looking up and around.

That time I'd heard it, too.

A very quiet scream.

Distant, but close enough to be picked up by the sharp ears of Sarge. You'd think a guy his age would have miniature amplifiers stuffed in his head, but his hearing was a thing of legend.

He glanced at me.

I nodded in response.

"Which way?"

He casually nodded at a building to our right.

"They're going to attack as soon as we walk in," he warned. *"Do you want to do that speed thing again or something?"*

"I can't use Haste *that fast in succession, but I can use* Freeze."

He squinted at me.

"What's that one do again?" he asked. *"Makes you like Ice Man or something?"*

I squinted back at him.

"No. It shuts down my emotions and pain receptors. Basically, think of it like me going into a state where I'm mentally cold as ice. I have no emotional blocks to stop me from ripping someone to shreds."

"So it makes you a killing machine?"

"Kind of."

"Can't have that, then." He rubbed his chin. *"Anything else?"*

"Just Superbone," I replied with a shrug. I then quickly added, *"It's what it sounds like, Sarge. You don't want me using that one, and I definitely don't want to use that one again. Dreadful experience."*

Sarge grunted. *"You're a really weird kid, junior. You know that?"*

"Comes with the territory of being an amalgamite, Sarge."

He glanced over at the building again and chewed his lip. The wheels were clearly turning. Walking through the front door was certainly a bad idea, but sometimes those were the ones that Sarge gravitated toward. His argument was that people were most surprised when you chose the dumbest option.

"Let's get in the car," he muttered. *"We'll leave the area and come through the back way."*

We got in and headed toward the gates.

I had my head on a swivel, looking at the fencing that ran down the property. It was pretty tall and the tops were pointy.

"They've got to have sentries around here, right?" I asked aloud, seeing no point in using the connector while in the privacy of the car.

"Nothing to worry about," he replied. "They're all kids. You just knock 'em out and that's that. Easy peasy."

Somehow I didn't think that would be true.

CHAPTER 53

$\mathcal{W}$e waited until dark and then Sarge took off through a mass of trees like he'd broken into this place before. That seemed odd considering he didn't have to break into the vampire compound.

"Where are we going?" I asked.

He stopped and gave me a look. "The vampire area, junior."

"I know that, Sarge," I groaned. "Where is this path leading us, though?"

"Tunnels," he said, moving forward again. "It's packed off in a hidden area. Old stuff. Got set up back during the Early Wars." He jumped over a small stream. "It was put here in case we got cornered. Gave us a way to flank or escape."

Not many people talked about the Early Wars. Apparently, this was before the Paranormal Police Department really got going. Factions took matters into their own hands during those dark days. According to the history I'd been forced to read in bootcamp, it was a mess of nonstop alliances and betrayals. Historians favored the example of the fae and pixies fighting the goblins. As soon as the fae and pixies got the upper hand over the goblins, the pixies turned on the fae and tried to knock them out while they were down. This, in turn, caused the fae to ally with the goblins and fight the pixies. One of the main issues with power is that it is incredibly addictive, even to the point of interrupting basic logic.

Sarge held out a hand and I came to a halt.

"*Go connector for now, kid,*" he commanded. "*I have to check on the area. Stay here and don't make a sound. I'll be right back.*"

I couldn't say I felt all that comfortable being left in the woods right next to the vampire compound. My uniform and badge might protect me in some places, but here they were easily buried with me.

Fortunately, I had decent eyesight in low lighting, so anything that got in close would be facing me with my eyes open.

"*Kid,*" Sarge said, causing me to jump, "*keep to the wall on your right and walk east. The area is clear and I've found the runes I was searching for. I'll need your help with them.*"

I followed along the wall, doing my best to avoid cracking sticks.

"*I don't know anything about runes,*" I said when I got in close to him. "*I can barely do a spell to make light.*"

"*Doesn't matter,*" he remarked. "*For now, I just need you to stand over there so I can use you as a ground for this energy rune.*"

"*Aren't those the ones that sting?*" I asked, moving to

where he told me to stand. *"I've heard that they really...argh!"*

The bolt of energy zipped along the ground and came up through my foot and straight into my groin. It hurt like shit. I'm talking the kind of pain you may feel if you sat directly on a 4-inch nail that was covered in acid.

It lasted about five seconds and then I fell over.

"You okay, junior?" Sarge asked, shaking me. *"That looked pretty nasty. Didn't expect it to travel over like that."* He scratched his head as he stared down at me. *"Well, I guess I kind of did expect that, but I thought it'd just pass right through you."*

"It did," I squeaked. *"In through my feet; out through my dick."*

"Ah, well," he coughed, *"that's no fun. Can you get up?"*

It took a fair bit of effort, but I finally managed to get to my feet. Sarge reached into his pocket and pulled out a flask.

"Healing," he said, handing it over. But then he stopped and pulled it back. *"Just a sip, now. We may need this when we go in there."*

I sipped and the radiating warmth of magic spread through my body, instantly relieving my pain.

"Better?"

"Yeah."

"Good," Sarge replied. *"Follow me."*

CHAPTER 54

The trip was slow because Sarge was doing his best to avoid the sentries. He made it clear that nobody would be expecting anyone to come through the hidden zone, especially because of the runes he'd just thwarted by using me.

"First thing we learn is how to bypass the runes so we can get in while keeping everyone else out."

"Wouldn't the wizard who made those runes know how to defeat them?" I asked after snapping a twig underfoot. *"Sorry."*

"Only if he could find them." He dropped down a bit as a sentry got within visual range. *"Contrary to popular belief, vampires aren't dumb."*

"Never thought they were," I replied. *"Arrogant, obnoxious, and shitty to mingle with, yes, but not dumb."* A little voice in the back of my head told me I needed to say a little more. *"Oh, uh, I mean in general. You're not arrogant, obnoxious, or shitty to mingle with, Sarge."*

"Thanks, junior," he muttered, frowning at me. *"Makes*

me feel swell to know you don't think of me as you do regular vampires."

"Uh..."

"Come on."

I took it upon myself to stay quiet as Sarge guided us through the area. Even though it was dark, I could see the building we were edging toward.

There were red lights on over the back door, and shadows played across the grass in various places. It looked like a party was underway. No music or anything, though, and nobody was talking.

As we closed in, I saw that this was because these weren't vampires walking around.

"Are those—" I started.

"Normals," Sarge finished. *"Yep."*

"They look like zombies."

"Ain't no such thing, kid," Sarge noted. *"Not anymore, anyway."*

Sometimes Sarge took me too literally. This often happened when we were in the middle of a precarious situation. Scanning the area and seeing a bunch of zombie-like forms, it was safe to say this was a precarious circumstance indeed.

"I count nineteen," Sarge announced. *"What have you got?"*

"Oh, uh..." I did a quick speed count and confirmed his number. *"Might be more inside, though."*

"Yeah," he agreed, *"but we only need one to prove what's going on."*

Great. So that was the plan. Snag one of the normals, escort them back to the precinct, and bring in the calvary.

"We just gotta hope they ain't tagged."

"Tagged?" I asked, not sure if I really wanted to know what that meant.

"It's like a branding," he replied as he gingerly reached out from the tree line and took one of the normals by the hand, guiding her back into the brush. *"Same thing they do to cattle."*

"Ah," I said, my stomach turning. *"That's kind of gross."*

"I'm sure cattle feel the same way."

He looked the woman over carefully. She didn't react in any way other than to stand there dull and listless. It was as though she'd been given a nice bag of pot brownies. The truth was that she was under the spell inflicted by the venom of a vampire. They would drain her blood for weeks until they finally decided to kill her. Of course, it wasn't easy to smuggle normals into the Netherworld, so she could be looking at many years of this dazed life as they continued feeding on her.

I shuddered at the thought.

"Free time is over," yelled a voice that sounded familiar. "Everyone inside. We wish to have dinner now."

"Maybell," Sarge said, holding on to the hand of the normal so she couldn't go anywhere. *"I knew she was up to something."*

"Yep," I agreed. *"Can we go now?"*

He nodded and began guiding the normal along with us. Once we got past the thinner trees though, it was obvious that the normal *was* branded.

Sarge and I knew this because she released a blood-curdling scream and passed out.

CHAPTER 55

There was no time to waste. Whistles were blown, commands were directed, and the sound of bodies rushing after us made it clear we were in the shit.

"Sling her over your shoulder and let's get the hell out of here," Sarge said, taking off like a man half his age.

"Why do *I* have to carry her?" I complained, even though she was pretty light.

"You're the junior officer," he grunted in response. "You get the coffee, take the verbal abuse, deal with shit I don't want to deal with, and carry venom-inflicted women over your shoulder while we run away. It's how things work."

Fact was that I had more stamina than Sarge did anyway.

The voices and rustling of our pursuers made it abundantly clear that we weren't going to reach the exit before they caught up to us. Sarge had to know that, but he kept his legs churning as best he could. Still, even with

JOHN P. LOGSDON & CHRISTOPHER P. YOUNG

the lady I had flung over my shoulder, I was about to zip right past him.

"They're gaining on us, Sarge."

"I know that," he panted. "We're going to have to fight, but I want to get as close to the exit as possible first."

"We can't fight all of them."

"I saw what you did at The Stipend, kid." He was wheezing now. "*Go to connector. I can't keep talking out loud while running.*"

"*I already told you that* Haste *is not something I can repeat this—*"

"*Then do that other one!*" he interrupted.

"*Superbone?*"

"*No, you idiot.* Chill *or whatever the hell you called it.*"

"*Freeze,*" I corrected. "*I'll end up killing a lot of them if I do that.*"

"*I think that's their plan for us anyway, junior, and better them to die than us, don't you think?*" He gave me a quick glance. "*Just do it.*"

"*I need time, Sarge. I can't just flip a switch.*"

I glanced back at the oncoming rush of vampires. At best, I'd have about twenty seconds, if I stopped now. It usually took a little longer than that to switch these things on.

"*Fine,*" he said. "*I'm going to stop running and hold them up. You go a little farther, put the body down, and get yourself set.*"

"*Don't get killed,*" I stated as he slowed.

I continued running until I heard Sarge call out for the vampires to stop where they were. Then I set the woman down carefully in the grass and closed my mind.

Going to *Haste* was fine because it just made me super fast, but *Freeze* kind of sucked. Imagine losing your empathy completely. You could take a life without it bothering you in the slightest. You became completely cold-hearted. There was no hesitation or caring at all. I could kill or I could merely injure. It didn't matter as long as I inflicted pain.

That was *Freeze*.

As the blanket of the skill slowly fell upon my mind, I could hear Sarge say that backup was already on the way.

Hopefully that was true.

My breath caught as *Freeze* took hold.

I slowly opened my eyes and found myself looking at the world as though it were nothing but a sepia canvas. The vividness of color was gone, as were stark contrasts.

Without pause, I stood and crunched through the brush back to where Sarge was doing his best to keep the vampires at bay. While I didn't give two shits about killing any one of those who were chasing us, I *was* able to know that killing Sarge was a bad thing. This wasn't empathy or caring, though. It was just simple logic. In other words, it wasn't like *Freeze* took away my ability to think, it just made me not care.

I strode straight past Sarge and ripped the throat out of the first vampire.

"Holy shit," was all the next nearest one could say before I ended his dreams and aspirations.

That's all it took for the vampires to start their attack.

I reached down and flipped my gun back to Sarge, along with a few magazines. He hated guns and I knew that, but I wasn't about to take on all the vampires without some assistance.

"Use it," I commanded just before grabbing a vampire by her head and snapping her neck. "I can't do this alone."

Yes, I was the junior officer here, but Sarge clearly saw the deadness in my eyes as he nodded and started unloading that gun like he was at the carnival trying to win a giant stuffed bear.

It helped to slow the vampires from charging at me.

Sort of.

They still came in, but most were shot before they reached me. Those who did reach me felt the sting of *Freeze*. Fortunately, Sarge was a good shot, and he knew precisely where to target a vampire. If all of them had been able to swarm me, I'd have been decimated, *Freeze* or not.

But it wouldn't last forever and once it wore off, I was going to hit the ground.

"*Go now, Sarge,*" I said through the connector, though it was difficult to use it in my state of mind.

"*Not a chance, junior.*"

Maybe I was just *too* logical when in this state, but I wasn't worried about my personal well-being in the least. Honestly, I didn't care about Sarge's either…or anyone here for that matter. But I *was* able to rationalize that the mission needed to be completed.

"*Both of us dying here does us no good,*" I noted without inflection.

"*True, but—*"

"*The mission comes first, Sarge.*"

"*Gah! Fine!*"

Another vampire's throat went missing as Sarge stepped up and handed me my gun.

"Use this and come with me. Your aim without emotion is going to be more effective than fighting them hand to hand."

Actually, he had a point there.

I took the gun and dropped ten vampires in only a few seconds. I then refilled the magazine with such speed that you'd have thought I was under the influence of *Haste*.

We ran as I picked off vampire after vampire.

I couldn't understand why they never brought guns to these parties, but I wasn't about to complain about that at the moment.

Sarge picked up the woman and continued on his merry way.

Three more shots dropped three more vampires.

"We're almost there," Sarge called through the connector.

"Freeze *is fading,"* I said, feeling suddenly woozy. *"I have maybe twenty seconds left."*

"Then run, junior!"

I tried, but the vampires had flanked us. There was no getting out of this without a full-on run.

"Drop the body, Sarge," I said, still cold in thought. *"We won't make it out with her."*

With a curse, he let her go and we kept rolling.

CHAPTER 56

We cleared the exit and burst through the tree line seconds before *Freeze* completely faded. I hit the ground, feeling dazed and confused.

Then I glanced back over my shoulder and saw a number of fanged faces stepping out toward us.

They already had the woman we were trying to save, and use as evidence. That sucked, but it wasn't as bad as the fact that we were now at their mercy.

That's when a massive line of lights lit up the area.

At first I thought it was just my mind finally giving in to the fact that I was going to pass out, but then I heard a voice over a PA.

"This is Chief Carter of the Netherworld PPD. Any one of you takes another step toward my officers and I'll have you gunned down."

Relief covered me milliseconds before my eyes rolled up into my head.

CHAPTER 57

*W*e were back at the station and I was seated in my little cubicle as Sarge raged across the aisle. He was pissed and I was reeling from the massive headache that using two amalgamite skills and downing elixirs will give you.

"So they didn't find anything?" I asked without opening my eyes.

"Scoured the entire compound while you were out," Sarge replied, slamming his hand on the desk with radiating effect. "Bastards either got rid of the normals or they hid them really well."

Unfortunately, without evidence taken directly from the scene, our hands were tied...and not in a succubus-playing-naughty kind of way either.

"My guess is they sent the normals back," I rasped, wishing that overhead lighting had never been invented. "Now that we're on to them, they won't risk it, no matter how yummy human blood tastes."

"At least not for a while," agreed Sarge before

slamming his desk once more. He glanced over at me. "Sorry, kid. I know your head hurts."

"A little." I chanced opening my eyes. "We at least got the guy I chased through the city, right?"

Sarge sighed. "Yeah, he'll be behind bars for a while, and you killed a buttload of vampires at the compound." He shook his head at me. "I wouldn't want to be on the other team when you're using your skills, junior. You're pretty deadly."

He said that with a look that said he was rather impressed.

I didn't feel proud about it, though. *Haste* was cool, but *Freeze* was just too callous. I could use it without killing, like I'd once done when I was chased by werewolves after my first week in the Netherworld, but killing is what it was intended for. At least, that's what I assumed. It wasn't like any of this came with an instruction manual, after all. I just stumbled upon things now and then. It wouldn't surprise me if I had more of these little gems living inside me, but until they revealed themselves, I wouldn't know.

"I'd prefer not to use them at all," I replied finally.

"I can imagine."

Sarge then cleared his throat and looked a bit uncomfortable.

"Something else wrong?" I asked.

"Look, kid," he answered after letting out a long breath, "you saved my hide out there tonight. I can usually take care of myself, but if you hadn't been there..." He paused and shrugged. "Well, anyway, I put in a few calls to some friends of mine topside, and when you graduate from here, you've got a spot on the Las Vegas Paranormal Police Department."

I blinked at him in disbelief.

"Seriously?"

He sniffed and shook his head.

"I can't see why you'd want to go up there, to be honest. When I was there, it was just a bunch of normals with some supers sprinkled in here and there." He crossed his arms. "You think supers are nasty? Wait until you see the horrible stuff normals do to each other, kid."

"I grew up topside, remember?"

"Oh, yeah," Sarge said. "Keep forgetting that. Well, then, I guess you already know what you're getting into."

And I did.

It wouldn't be great living topside, but it gave me the chance to blend in most of the time. Not with supers, no, but normals didn't know I wasn't human. I'd rather be left alone ninety percent of the time and deal with supers ten percent than the other way around.

"Thanks for doing that, Sarge," I said sincerely.

"Yeah, yeah, yeah," he said, waving at me. "Don't go getting all sentimental on me or I'll have to kick your ass."

I cracked a smile at him.

"You can always come up and visit sometime, you know? Maybe you just needed to have someone show you the place who knows it."

"Thanks, kid, but no thanks." He stared at the papers on his desk. "You're my last junior cop. Once you're gone, I'm buying a little place outside of town and living off my pension. I've had enough excitement to last me ten lifetimes."

And with that, Sarge got back to work, filling out forms and cursing a lot.

I still had a number of months to serve out as a junior cop, but I was damn glad to have a mentor like Sarge to point me down the right path.

He gave a shit, and because of that, I was learning to give a shit, too.

"Sarge," I said after a few more moments of suffering under the lights, "I'm going to take off a little early and get some rest, if that's okay."

"You've earned it," he replied without looking back. I stood up and started out, when he said, "Might want to steer clear of that vampire guard you tried to hit on, junior."

"Huh?"

"I saw you give her your card," he said, raising an eyebrow at me.

"She threw it away."

He rubbed his neck and leaned back in his chair.

"Something tells me she'll dig it back out of the trash the next chance she gets."

"Why would you think that?"

"Just a hunch, kid," he replied with a smirk. "Just a hunch."

One of these days I hoped I'd get hunches like Sarge. In the meantime, I was going to do all I could to learn from him.

If all went well, I'd be a full cop in the Las Vegas PPD inside of a year. That was both exciting and scary. Then again, how bad could it be? It wasn't like I was going to have to worry about being a chief anytime soon or anything.

I laughed a little to myself and then grabbed my head and winced.

"Good night, Sarge."

"G'nite, kid."

∾

The End

∾

Thanks for Reading

If you enjoyed this book, would you please leave a review at the site you purchased it from? It doesn't have to be a book report... just a line or two would be fantastic and it would really help us out!

John P. Logsdon
www.JohnPLogsdon.com

John was raised in the MD/VA/DC area. Growing up, John had a steady interest in writing stories, playing music, and tinkering with computers. He spent over 20 years working in the video games industry where he acted as designer, programmer, and producer on many online games. He's now a full-time comedy author focusing on urban fantasy, science fiction, fantasy, Arthurian, and GameLit. His books are racy, crazy, contain adult themes and language, are filled with innuendo, and are loaded with snark. His motto is that he writes stories for mature adults who harbor seriously immature thoughts.

Christopher P. Young

Chris grew up in the Maryland suburbs. He spent the majority of his childhood reading and writing science fiction and learning the craft of storytelling. He worked as a designer and producer in the video games industry for a number of years as well as working in technology and admin services. He enjoys writing both serious and comedic science fiction and fantasy. Chris lives with his wife and an ever-growing population of critters.

CRIMSON MYTH PRESS

Crimson Myth Press offers more books by this author as well as books from a few other hand-picked authors. From science fiction & fantasy to adventure & mystery, we bring the best stories for adults and kids alike.

www.CrimsonMyth.com